A Messenger and Bad Tidings!

..m not sure why bad news has to pick nice, ..unny spring days to arrive and alter perfectly ..ontented lives. But I had noticed that Mother ..ad been wearing all three of her special crystals .. the last few days, and usually she wore only ..he one. She had also been casting frequent ..ances up the north road, outside the gates of ..afret Hall that led to Princestown. I did too, ..ng caught her nervousness, but it was she in .. nd who saw the messenger, beating his lath- .. and weary horse up the long drive…

Other Cosmos Books

IF WISHES WERE HORSES

by
Anne McCaffrey

COSMOS BOOKS

IF WISHES WERE HORSES
October 2007

Published by

Dorchester Publishing Co., Inc.
200 Madison Avenue
New York, NY 10016

in collaboration with Wildside Press, LLC

Copyright © 1998, 2007 by Anne McCaffrey

Cover painting copyright © 2006 by Charles Bernard

Cover design by Garry Nurrish.
Typeset by Swordsmith Productions

ISBN-10: 0-8439-5912-6
ISBN-13: 978-0-8439-5912-3

The name "Cosmos Books" and the Cosmos logo are the property of Wildside Press, LLC.

Printed in the United States of America.

As it was then, so it is now.

IF WISHES
WERE HORSES

Of course, many people in our small county village sought advice and help from my mother long before the War started because she was quite wise as well as gifted with a healing touch. Often, day and night, we would hear the front door knocker—shaped like a wyvern it was, with a stout curled tail—bang against the brass sounding circle. That summons was undeniable, echoing through the Great Hall and up the stairs. There was no sleeping once someone started pounding. Sometimes they didn't pound but tapped, quietly but insistently, so that one was awakened more by the muted repetition than the noise. From the time I was twelve, I got roused quite as often as my mother did. Of course, I was also able to turn over and go back to sleep, which my mother could not.

"Those of us who *can* help, *should* not deny it to others," my mother was apt to say, usually to still my father's grumblings. "I'll just see what I can do for them."

"Day *and* night?" my father would demand in an exasperated or frustrated tone of voice.

However, he was such a heavy sleeper that he was rarely disturbed when she slipped from the huge oak four-poster bed to answer the summons. As I grew older and she began to rely on me to assist her from time to time, I realized that he never answered the nocturnal rapping, though occasionally Mother would send me to wake him to help us. What I never did figure out—then—

was how she knew, on our way down the main staircase, that she would *need* his protection to answer that particular summons.

"Oh, it's nothing mysterious, Tirza love," Mother told me. "If you listen, you'll learn quick enough the difference in the *sound* of the knocking. That can tell me a lot."

It took me nearly two years before I could differentiate between the hysterical, the urgent, or the merely anxious kind of rapping.

Mother's ability to have some sort of a solution to almost any problem had become somewhat legendary in our part of the Principality. She had a fund of general knowledge, an unfailing sympathy augmented by common sense, and a remarkable healing touch.

"Much of the time, Tirza, they only need someone who *listens,* and they end up knowing their *own* solutions. You may well have inherited the family failing, love," she went on with a sigh. When she saw my stunned expression, she had added cheerfully, "But we won't know that for a while yet. Oh, it could be worse, know. You could have inherited Aunt Simona's teeth."

That was quite enough to send me into the giggles.

"Oh, I am terrible!" And she rolled her eyes in mock-penitence. "However could I be so unkind as to mention Aunt Simona's teeth! I may have no jam with tea tonight." Her lovely eyes twinkled. "Now do be a *good* child and get me some clean bottles for this lotion I've just made for Mistress Chandler."

Nonetheless, I never heard anyone, not even Father, refer to Mother's ministrations as failings. Except perhaps Aunt Simona, who had more than large, protruding front teeth to make her unlovable. Mother also had an unerring ability to know who was speaking from the heart, telling the truth, and who might be unwilling to own up to the consequences of his or her actions. Father would invariably delay his magisterial sittings until she could join him, though her participation was confined to sitting quietly at one end of the table. Strangers would try to prevaricate or settle blame elsewhere, but she was never deceived in any particular. She and Father must have worked out some sort of private signals, for she never spoke at these sessions, merely listened. Father was the one who pounced on the culprit and would be in possession of details that would stun the miscreant, often into a terrified and more accurate account of what had happened. So, if Lady Talarrie Eircelly was known for her wisdom and hearing, Lord Emkay Eircelly was equally renowned for fair and firm justice.

During the day, village women were more apt to come to the kitchen door, slipping into the big warm room with all its marvelous aromas and giving Liwy some hint of what their problem was. A cup of tea and a 'morsel to eat with it'—anything from a slab of cake or plate of fresh sweet biscuits—would be instantly served by our Liwy. Even if that had not been Mother's standing order, Liwy was the sort of person who knew the soothing properties of nice hot tea and a treat or two. Some folk eased in quietly, almost apologetically: others would already be in tears and found themselves comforted by Liwy's ample self. The shyer men would come to the kitchen, too, murmuring about not wishing to disturb her ladyship.

"Which same," Liwy would say tartly when she sent Tess to guide them to wherever Mother was at that time of day, "is exactly what they want to do and why they came. Mostly," Liwy added, banging her pots and lids about or doubling the energy with which she did her present task, "all they need is to hear pure common sense. If they'd stop and *think,* which a body should be able to do, they'd see how to handle things. Seems to me as if they have to have Authority give 'em the word. Wear milady out, so they will." This threat would be accompanied by one of her gusty sighs. "And that's not fair on her. What'll happen if they've wore her out so much she's unable to see to all the things she has to do in any one day or another?"

"Could they wear Mother out?" my brother, Tracell, asked, startled. We had seen the latest arrival, for he had skulked about the herb garden, getting up the courage to come to the kitchen door. And we, dreadful children that we were, had followed—just in case there might be something we could wheedle out of Liwy when she had finished dispensing hospitality to him. "I heard her tell Aunt Rachella that it was having babies that wears her out."

"Most it would, the way she has them," Liwy had said with a snort. "Two at a time."

"Catron came by herself," Tracell reminded her.

Liwy humphed. "Well-bred ladies like your dear mother ought not to be having twins. That's for common folk, not *ladies!*"

"Why not?"

"Now, Lady Tirza, that's not for me to tell you and you will kindly forget...what was just said. I wouldn't want anyone saying I'd said a word against Lady Talarrie." And she passed us the plate of lady cakes.

"Mother's not having another set of twins, is she?" Tracell demanded anxiously.

"I should hope not!" Liwy said so firmly that we knew she must, indeed, know.

Any way, Mother had always told us, her oldest, when new babies were coming. She'd ever known that Catron was coming by herself. Then she had Andras and Achill. And, when Father came back from the Miriseng Campaign, she told us that the next pair would be girls, Diana and Desma.

"So, don't you fret, young Tracell," Liwy said, putting the now empty plate in the sink, "about your lady mother. She's got strength for seven and sense for a dozen. Just do your best not to add to the trials and tribulations everyone else brings her."

"She's *our* mother," Tracell said stoutly.

"For which you should be eternally grateful. Now out of my kitchen! I can hear her ladyship's step, and you've no need to be here to embarrass young Sten. Like as not, she'll have to bring him through here to the still room, so make yourselves scarce."

As we could hear my mother's voice with the phrase that ever seemed to be on her lips, "I'll just see what I can do about that right now ..." we were out the door in a flash.

"I'll see what I can do about it," was Mother's habitual response to most matters brought to her attention.

In itself, the phrase was unusually effective. For instances, the day Tray fell off his pony and broke one of the bones in his forearm, her calmly confident, "Now I'll just see what I can do about this…" cut him off mid-howl even though she had just given a careful yank on his wrist. I had heard the grate of the bones as they settled into line again. We used our two riding crops as temporary splints, tied on with the flounce of Mother's petticoat. Tray was too surprised and— I must say—rather brave to forego any further outcry, though he was dreadfully pale until we got him back to the house and into his bed.

I'm not sure why bad news has to pick nice, sunny spring days to arrive and alter perfectly contented lives. But I had noticed that Mother had been wearing all three of her special crystals for the last few days, and usually she wore only the one. She had also been casting frequent glances up the north road, outside the gates of Mallafret Hall that led to Princestown. I did too, having caught her nervousness, but it was she in the end who saw the messenger, beating his lathered and weary horse up the long drive. Immediately she summoned my father from his study, sent me to get ale, bread and cheese from the kitchen, and ordered Tray to collect one of our fast and durable hunters from the stables.

"Bring up that bright bay, the one you say has no bottom to him," she said. "Bridled."

"No saddle?"

"The messenger will use his own."

"What messenger?" asked Tray, because the thick trunks of the oak trees that lined the drive briefly masked the oncoming rider.

"The one on his way up the avenue. Go! Now!"

No one argued with that tone in Mother's voice, and Tray raced for the stables as I ran to the kitchen. So we all appeared, along with Father, just as Prince Sundimin's courier, his face gaunt with fatigue, as exhausted as the lathered mount who staggered up our drive, reached the wide front stairs.

His message, while brief, was momentous, announcing that Prince Refferns of Effester had started a war with our Principality. Our good Prince Sundimin perforce had to raise an army to defend our cities and lands. All liegemen were to honor their oath to their prince.

"Lord Eircelly," the herald gasped, "muster your men with all possible speed." Then he blinked with gratitude at the tankard of ale, which I held up to him while Mother gestured he should moisten his dry throat before continuing. "Deepest thanks, milady. Milord, the prince bade me to deliver into your very hands this message," and he handed over a square of parchment, "and to assure you that the matter is of the gravest urgency." He then tipped the tankard, drinking a good half of its contents. "I must also beg the favor of a replacement mount, milord," he continued, "since I have far yet to go before I finish my assigned task." Stiffly, he swung his right leg over the cantle and would have fallen against the horse had not my father, leaping forward, immediately lent a hand to steady him.

"The favor is already granted, I see," my father said at his driest, with a glance at Tray, who was leading a bright bay from the stable yard.

"Sit, sir, and eat while we change the saddle," Mother said and all but pushed the messenger onto the broad wing of the shallow stairs of Mallafret Hall.

"Very good, my thanks, milady, milord. I was urged not to stop..."

"Changing horses is scarcely a stop, my man," my father said, "and you must restore yourself or you'll not go much further on. Have you to ride all the way to the sea?"

The weary man nodded, his mouth too full of bread and cheese to speak.

"The road is good, the way is clear, and the sunshine will hold," Mother said.

By then, Tray and Father had changed the saddle to the bay's back. As the man made two attempts to swing aboard his fresh mount, Mother tucked a second loaf in the saddlebag and urged him to eat as he rode onward.

"The bay is genuine," Father said. "Trust him. God's speed!"

Father stepped back and the man immediately kneed his fresh horse into a canter. He gave one wave as he turned right at the gate toward his next stop and the distant sea.

"For that matter," Tray said, "he could probably sleep on the bay and he'd keep going until he's reined in. And you, my brave lad?" Tray asked the splay-legged, drooping headed mount whose breath came in wheezing gasps. "Shall we save you?"

Father looked up from breaking the seal of the message with all its dangling official princely stamps.

"I shan't expect the impossible, Tracell," my father said, gently, "but I'd hazard that he's one of those marvelous plains' Cirgassians and worth the effort."

"A Cirgassian?" Tray exclaimed, really looking at the exhausted animal.

"Just look at the ears, the fine head, the deep barrel... if we can save him, we should try. Do see what you can do." Then, having broken the seals, his eyes flicked through the usual florid opening paragraphs to the important part of how many men he must bring in answer to this muster.

"Last year's bad season in Effester has made

Prince Refferns envious of our prosperity?" my
mother asked.

"As you so often do, my dear Talarrie, you
have hit upon the crux of the matter. We are
enjoined to give our liege prince the service and
support due him as quickly as is humanly possible."

"Then the Shupp is low from the drought?"
Mother asked.

"Correct as usual, my prescient love. Tracell,
see this poor fellow stabled in the thickest bed of
straw you and Surgey can make, and groom him
into such comfort as he may enjoy in his sad condition. Or would you rather take the drum to the
village and announce the muster?"

To my brother's credit, the care of a horse of
such a distinguished breed ranked first in impor-
tance. So it fell to Sir Minshall as Seneschal, with
young Emond beating the drum, to speed to the
village square to announce an immediate muster
and set the disaster bell to peeling out its summons. There were plenty of young lads in the village to send to apprise outlying farms, beyond
the range of even that melodious bell, of the

emergency and the haste that must be made in answer to the summons. Mother, Liwy, and I helped Father pack his saddlebags, add an almost unneeded burnish to his armor, for Emond was not careless with his duties as equerry, and roll up his travel blankets and gear.

Father immediately dispatched an advance party of armed troopers and appointed dawn by the next morning as the moment of departure for the larger force. Thirty mounted knights there were, plus fifty foot soldiers, the muster that our prince required of my father from his oath of fealty. Father looked very pleased with the speed at which all had assembled, ready to travel. More was in readiness than could have been expected for all it had been decades since the prince had had to call upon his liegemen to defend his borders.

"Scarce twenty hours between the call to arms and our response," Father murmured to my mother and me, for Tracell now held the bridle of Father's heavy-boned war steed in the courtyard. In the courtyard and spilling beyond the graveled avenue, digging up the lawn with heavy boots and shod hooves, were the others, banners unfurled and faces grim.

"Speed is surely a requirement in any muster," my mother said proudly and lifted her face for his farewell kiss.

"I didn't think to assemble so smartly, though," my father said, holding her in his arms.

"I am not the only competent one in this Hall," she said in an attempt at levity.

Did I see tears in my father's eyes at this moment of farewell? Possibly mine were overfull as well for I was frightened. All the soldiery looked so brave in their fine uniforms, all the metal shiny and dangerous.

Everyone who could have come to see our brave men depart, lining the avenue where they could, and the northern road as far as we could see.

"I can leave all else in your hands, my dear Competence," my father said to my mother as he stamped his feet into his heavy boots, the ones with extra flaps above the knee to prevent sword cuts to his thighs. The other armsmen of Mallafret Hall were no less efficient in preparing themselves and had organized baggage wains, pack animals, ammunition and additional horses.

"Had you a warning you kept to yourself, Talarrie?" I heard my father softly ask my mother though they did not know I was within hearing distance.

Mother's hand went unerringly to the crystals she wore on the long chains about her neck.

"I'd knowledge of a sort, so I thought to have everyone check their equipment. We can also be thankful that the year gave us a good spring to plant in."

"My wise and lovely Talarrie," and there was a pause as they clung together.

"You will be safe, my love," she added as she stepped back, fingers tight about the crystals.

So the troop moved at a smart trot, the foot soldiers hanging onto stirrup leathers to keep up with the mounted troops. They were cheered out of the gates of the Hall, and relatives and friends fell in behind the troop, accompanying them well up the main road to Princestown. With unbecoming pride, I hoped that they would be first to join the main army of Prince Sundimin.

"When will they come back, Mother?" I asked when our brave troop was so far away that we could not longer see the dust the horses kicked up. I had been very much aware of the sorrow in my mother's eyes and the tense grip of her fine fingers on her crystals.

"Not soon enough, Tirza," Mother said with a sad little smile. "And not all who left here this morning." Then she gave me a little smile, cupping my head in her hand. "But *he* will return." She released the crystals, picked up her skirts, and went back into the house.

"Surely the war won't take long, will it, mother?" asked my brother. After the scurry to get everyone prepared, he looked disgruntled. At fourteen he was much too young to be mustered with the men and, as my father's heir, he could not even go as drummer as had fourteen-year-old Riaret, the smith's lad. Tray adored our father, as indeed he should, and while some of his lessons included the studying of old battles and sieges and such like, he certainly ought to have known that wars had a habit of taking far longer than the most optimistic opinion. But then, Father always won the mock engagements they invented in three days, four at most.

I knew before my mother answered that the war would not be short or a four-day rout: one of those awful premonitions to which I was prone. I tried very hard not to let them insert themselves in my mind, but they appeared as they chose. Like waking one morning, when I was ten, and knowing that Father's best stallion had impaled himself on a stake in the top field and bled to death. Or knowing that my youngest sister, Desma, was choking on a pea that had fallen out of her rattle. But Mother had known, too, and reached her in time to scoop out the impediment and open the path of air to her lungs.

"The war will take whatever time is required to end it," Mother told Tray, which was not the answer he wanted. "Do close your mouth, Tray. You wouldn't want to swallow a fly."

I also knew what else worried my twin, but then we were closely bonded in our twinship. My father had promised Tracell the pick of the young horses for his sixteenth birthday, one that he could train on his own. Right now our fields and stables were virtually empty of all but brood mares and the one stallion too old for battle. And the foundered Cirgassian.

"If the war lasts very long, there won't be a horse for me on my sixteenth birthday," Tracell complained as we followed Mother inside Mallafret Hall.

"If that should be the case," Mother said cheerfully, "I'll be sure to do something about it, my love. You *will* have the promised steed on your birthday. I'll see to that."

That was reassurance enough for Tracell, who lost his worried frown and quite pranced.

"Of course," Mother went on with a sly glance at him, "you must now share with me many of the duties your father undertakes, for I shall need a strong man at my side during the times to come."

"But Sir Minshall is Seneschal," my brother said.

"And he is very well known to have been a fine soldier, winning many battles ... in his day," my mother replied. "He will look finely fierce if I am required to give audience to men of rank, but it is on you whom I rely: you and Tirza."

"Yes, of course, mother," we said in chorus.

So that was one reason that I *knew* that we were in for a long separation from Father, which increased my original foreboding.

I said nothing but clasped Mother's hand tightly when hers closed on mine. So she knew that I knew and was warning me not to speak. Unlike Tracell, who speaks without thought most of the time, I somehow have the sense to know when to keep silent. Of course, with such a collection of brothers and sisters all demanding attention, I had little opportunity to get words in edgewise. Tracell had always talked for the pair of us, even when we were learning to speak and I had been content to let him. Until the time I heard Nurse fretting to my mother that she worried that I talked so seldom.

"Ah, but when she does speak, she speaks in good sentences and to a purpose," my mother had said, stroking my hair and hugging me. "My gracious silence," she added, smiling at me, and her smiles were worth all the words in the world.

"If you say so, milady," my nurse had replied, still dubious.

After that, I made an effort to talk, though sometimes the only things to be said were so obvious that it was almost a waste of breath to mention them. Why comment on the obvious? Like a sunny day. Or a good soaking rain to encourage crops and flowers to grow. Or how well the youngest twins were doing.

By the time I was twelve, I learned that some

people would say one thing—as often my father's tenants did—and yet you could hear what they should have said, or wanted to say and didn't dare. There were times when I knew I should mention the disparity to Father or Mother. Sometimes I did not. Unless, of course, Mother took me to one side and asked, "What does my gracious silence think?" Which meant it was proper for me to speak out.

Unlike Tracell's anxiety to be given a fine horse for his sixteenth birthday, I had always known that the present that would be mine when I became sixteen was safely in Mother's locked chest, hidden behind the fireplace in her room. I *knew* that the crystal had been there since my birth, for it was a distaff tradition that crystals were given to each daughter on the occasion of her sixteenth birthday. Even the ones for my other sisters—Catron, Diana and Desma—were safely in keeping. (Mother had known the outcome of each of her pregnancies: that my next youngest sister, Catron, would arrive by herself. Followed by two more boys, Andras and Achill, then Diana and Desma.)

The rest of that auspicious day when Father answered the call of his prince was odd for we were both elated at how quickly the muster had been made and then suddenly bereft of important tasks to be done. I did help Tray with the Cirgassian. He had the most delicate pointy ears—still drooping in his exhaustion. He would need much care if he were to survive.

"I've never seen a Cirgassian before," Tray remarked to Surgey as they gently groomed the last of the hardened lather and dirt from its flanks. It stood, head down in the stable, golden straw up to its belly. Tray would offer it water from time to time but kept the portions small.

"Worth our effort, sor," Surgey agreed.

"Maybe you'll cure him well enough to be ridden again," I suggested, though I wasn't all that sure of it. It would be very good for Tray if the animal recovered. For my brother was much too long in the leg anymore for his pony.

"Well, I shall certainly see what I can do about this fellow," Tray said, hands on his hips. He sounded so like Mother that I stared at him until he was aware of my astonishment and gave me a grin. "After all, Mother only does what needs to be done and I know what needs to be done with him."

Which was, of course, the exact and complete truth, and so I was quite as happy to help my twin as I would be to assist Mother.

Of course, as messages began to arrive from the battle lines, there was much more to think about. Father's troops had responded so expeditiously that they shamed the musters of other villages on the way into doubling their efforts to swell the ranks at Princestown. And thus our Prince Sundimin was able to meet the initial attack of the aggressor, Prince Refferns of Effester. That prince, thinking to find an easy mark in our Principality, did not. In fact, he was pushed back across the River Shupp, which was the boundary between our Principalities. If my father's messages to us singled out the most valiant of our townsmen, and those whose bravery had cost them their lives, the messages the heralds proclaimed suggested that our father's leadership had been the primary cause of our success. Prince Sundimin was an older, cautious man who had not previously had to take up arms to defend his borders. I could see that the 'games' my father had played with Tracell and those he had inveigled into their maneuvers had been far more beneficial than many such other pastimes.

But the war dragged on because Prince Refferns, deprived of an easy victory, employed mercenaries to strengthen his weakened lines, certain from the ease and force with which his army had been beaten back across the Shupp that Sundimin would press the advantage. So, perforce, Sundimin had to make alliances with other

Princedoms, west and south of our Principality, to be sure that Effester, now advised by professional soldiers, did not outflank him.

"We can see them across the wide river," Father wrote Mother—she always read his infrequent letters to us (though perhaps not every word he wrote) "and they us, but there isn't a bridge left now for many leagues on either side of the Shupp. All have been burned so do not look for the usual supplies from the east. Be sure to gather in the harvest and preserve it well."

Mother had not needed that advice. The day after Father and his company had left, she had distressed Siggie the head gardener to the point of tears when she made him dig up all the flowers—save for the roses—and plant vegetables, using the arbors for beans, tomatoes, squash and peas. She sent word to all our villagers that they were to do likewise, and had the gamekeepers increase the snares for rabbit and coney, and for pheasant and grouse, and culled the deer of the old or lame which would have been allowed to die as their time came. She had us all out in the ornamental lakes of the formal gardens, deepening the long rectangles so that we, like the farmers, could stock pond waters with river tench, bream and carp. The wood lakes received her attention as well, and the forest streams so that we had racks and racks of drying fish while the cooper's apprentices were increased to twenty as the orders for kegs, barrels and tuns came in. I have never spent such a busy summer, but somehow Mother had the knack of making the work seem both novel and one more way of keeping Father and all our friends in his company well supplied when winter came.

At harvest time, while the battles seemed to seesaw across the Shupp by way of pontoon bridges or other craft tied together, even the oldest villagers were put to work, sitting down if they could not stand or glean, or perched on high stools to flail the seed from the full heads of the crop. She had the hedgerows scoured for useful herbs, which were dried against need. And because we children worked beside her and the villagers, no complaint came to our ears as we worked all the long summer hours God gives a day in our latitude.

"Sure'n' we could feed all Prince Sundimin's armies with what we've here," someone remarked.

"Sure'n what else are we doing this for?" was the doughty response.

So it surprised no one when my father sent a letter asking for what supplies could be spared, for the armies were wintering along the river Shupp, neither force willing to withdraw. And more princelings, further down the river, all the way to the seaport, began to eye each other across the broad Shupp. Since Mallafret had huge, dry cellars, much had been stored with us as well as in the three great village barns. The last of our horses pulled the wagons. Our farmers themselves accompanied the drays pulled by their oxen, determined to return with the beasts no matter what. They managed, but only because Father sent an escort along with them to be sure of their return. And because meat—even haunches of our venison—had been part of our offerings, the oxen did not have to be sacrificed.

In one exception, Mother had also had us older five children secrete a portion—a tithe, she called it—in the deepest and darkest cellars of Mallafret where few would look for anything other than seemingly blank walls. And she enjoined us to secrecy.

"You mean the war is going on and on, don't you, Mother?" Tracell said gloomily, for we were both now fifteen.

"I said I'd see what I can do about your birthday horse, Tracell," she said firmly.

"Mother, you're as clever as you can stare," Tray said with a certain maturity in his voice— for his voice was now a firm tenor, "but with so many horses needed by the army, however will there be one for me? Besides Courier who can barely walk without wheezing." For that was what we had named the Cirgassian who had somehow survived his ordeal.

"I intend to see what I can do." And she walked off on some other of the many duties that were her never-ending responsibility in Father's absence.

"Tray, I could kick you," I said, keeping my voice low but meaning him harm, "to doubt Mother so."

He gave me a long look. "I have every respect for our mother, Tirza, but there are some things even she will find it difficult to provide in these times."

The unmistakable sound of cannon and the discharge of other weapons wakened us one cold wintry morning just before Solstice. While rousing the rest of us to close and bar the shutters of the all-too-many windows of Mallafret Hall, Mother sent Tray to see what had happened and to offer shelter to the villagers. The barrage was

at least sporadic and the Shupp, half a mile beyond the village, was full of wintry snow and
rain, running too rapidly to allow ice to form—
and thus preventing easy access from our enemy.
Tray, hauling his long legs up almost to his chin,
galloped bareback off on the pony, who was
speedier of foot than the poor wind-broken
Courier.

"While he's gone, we must see what we can do
to protect ourselves should the enemy somehow
cross the river and seek to pillage," Mother said
and briskly gave her orders.

"But what *can* we do, milady?" Sir Minshall
demanded, for Mallafret was a manor house, not
a castle, though it was stoutly built of the native
golden stone.

"Sir Minshall, we may be women and young
folk, but there is much that we all can do. And
will!" she said so staunchly that he blushed with
shame. "We have lances, we have the old long
rifles—and powder and shot for them, if I am not
mistaken. We have crossbows and quarrels from
an even earlier war, and bows and arrows even
now used to hunt deer. We have heights from

which we can pour boiling oil on those who might seek to enter Mallafret. First, girls, go shutter every window. Sir Minshall, Surgey, Siggie, be so good as to pull the heaviest chests across the doorways. Liwy, Tess, Tirza, take our largest kettles and boil oil. Not the new pressings. The old will do as well, and be sure to have lighted torches so we give them a good roasting once they've been soaked in oil."

"We have so many doors, milady," Sir Minshall said anxiously.

"And quite likely as many nails. Fetch the stout planks we use to clean the ceilings and refresh the chandeliers. I'll see what else I can do."

When I helped carry the first of the cauldrons up the many flights of stairs to be settled just over the main entrance, I could see that the village was afire. Leaving Tess and Liwy to arrange the 'welcome' blessing of hot oil, I raced to tell Mother.

"Tray will know to bring the survivors back to us. Let us devoutly hope some have weapons," she said. "Stuff my lavender scarf through the shutters above the secret door, for that is the only one unsealed. Tray will have sense enough to see what is meant by it."

"No one can have used it in hundreds of years," I said, for although we of the Eircellys knew of its existence, not even Tray or I would have dared use it—for fear someone might oversee us.

Mother favored me with a smile. "Not used, to be sure, but kept oiled and passable. One never does know when something like that will be needed."

Somehow that forethought of hers turned my fear to resolution. Whatever we must do to secure Mallafret from pillage and destruction *would* be done and be sufficient to our need.

Tray did return, four small children sitting numbly on his pony, and behind him, carrying what they had been able to save, walked many of the village women. Luckily the pony fit through the secret door, though first the children had to be taken from his back.

"The men have all stayed to defend what

homes remain," Tray said, his face covered with smuts and one hand blistered. He also carried a musket someone had supplied him. "But Effestrians cannot cross," he added fiercely. "Not that they didn't try, but they did not take into account the current and have been carried so far below us, toward the first rapids, that I doubt they will survive the journey or make another attempt. Farms are sending reinforcements to assist us, so I shall return now, having discharged my duty to our people."

"Only after I have seen what I can do about your hand, my son," my mother said proudly and shortly attended his injury. As he left, taking the pony with him out the secret door, I saw her hand clutching the crystals. She saw my gaze on her action and nodded solemnly. "He will be all right," she murmured before she drew me back to help her attend others. "Now let us see what we can do to settle these people."

"Yes, Mother," I said, following.

"Who is hurt?" she called in a voice that could be heard across the Great Hall, now filled with weeping and fretting folk. "Tirza, we will need hot water and tea, and perhaps a tot of something stronger to restore spirits."

"Let us do that, milady," the cooper's wife said, stepping forward. She had served at the hall before her marriage and knew where things were kept.

"That is an excellent thought, Merva," Mother said, "much appreciated. Tirza, if you will separate the injured from the sound, then we can continue with our preparations to defend Mallafret."

"I doubt they would be able to come ashore, milady," Merva said stoutly. "Not only is the current swift but the river itself is filled with... *things*...that bump and slither and can easily overturn the silly rafts they made. An' as soon as the first cannon went, so my man took the last horse with four good legs and rode to summon such as are left to come to our aid."

"Well done, but Quiman has always been sensible," my mother said approvingly and Merva preened before she recalled herself to the tasks at hand.

With all the heavy cauldrons full of hot oil, every other pan of size in the kitchen had to be used to cook a morning porridge while other women continued with the bread which Liwy had set to rise. By the time all stomachs were full of a warm and nourishing meal, Mother had a good idea of the destruction wrecked on the village from talking to those as she served them. Only two of the cannon balls had landed on targets, yet so many cottages had been built butt-on-butt that almost the whole riverside row, including the inn, the school, and the church had burned. That left over a hundred and fifty without shelter and deprived of most of their belongings—beds and clothes being the most critical of the losses in this depth of winter. And the Solstice but a week away. Handcrafts made for the celebration, new clothing, and other gifts as well as foodstuffs hoarded for a good feasting were likewise so much ash.

"I'll have to see what I can do," Mother said, fingering her crystals, and I did wonder how she would manage to rise to this disaster. Especially with Mallafret not yet secure from attack.

Mid afternoon a troop raced up the avenue led by sons of nearby estates, too young yet to be mustered—although if the war continued much longer, they too would be called up. Tray, of course, rode in the lead, proudly astride his pony, his legs stuck out in front of him so they wouldn't drag on the ground.

Although the sight of Tray reassured both Mother and me, we nevertheless greeted the new arrivals with such men as we had left and three of the largest women. Sir Minshall had been unable to stoop sufficiently to use the secret door but he manned one of the long rifles bristling through the slits of the shutters.

"The Effestrian force perished at the rapids, mother," Tray said, dismounting by the expedient of standing up on his long legs and letting the pony walk out from under him. His face was filthy and he had scrapes on his face and arms where the sleeves were torn, but his blistered hand was still protected by a very dirty bandage. "I've left pickets both north and south," and he pointed, "and we met a scouting party from Princestown who came to see how far south the Effestrians managed to push. We are advised that Prince Monteros is moving his forces north as fast as he can. Though some say," and now Tray sounded quite cynical, "that he is not apt to pursue anyone past his own borders." He had been moving towards her as he spoke and now embraced her. "It's all right now, Mother. Mallafret is safe."

"And you will be hungry, no doubt," Mother said, smiling as if he had been on an outing with friends. "We can certainly do something about that!"

Tray waved his good hand diffidently. "If you will pack it up for us, please. We will quarter ourselves in the village to be sure the enemy does not return, seeking the cannon which we caused to fall into the Shupp."

"Oh!"

I believe that was the first time I ever saw my mother at a complete loss for words. Then she gripped Tray by the arms, her face beaming with pride. "So it wasn't running that pony through the woods that caused you so many scratches?"

"Indeed not, milady," said the scion of another family, grinning from ear to ear. "Thought Tray's plan a capital one, since most of us know the ways of our river and how to cross safely. I am Keffine, son of Lord Hyland." He gave as courtly a flourish as if he had been clad in silks instead of torn and soot-smutted leathers.

"How are you for ammunition?" Mother asked.

"Sufficient, milady," Keffine said, tapping bulky saddlebags.

"Much of the village is burned," she added.

"We'll fare well, milady," the scion said and jerked his head at Tray. "We must settle in for the night and set our watches."

"All are safe here?" Tray asked, looking at the tightly boarded house.

"We shall be quite safe." My mother kissed his cheek, a maternal salute that he bore with considerably more poise than he would once have managed.

The pony had come back to stand beside him, and swinging his leg wide and across the little beast, Tray reined him about and led his tatterdemalion troop back down the avenue.

"He deserves a proper horse," I heard my mother mutter as we made our way back to the

secret door—scarcely a secret now, but useful
with every other entrance to the house barri-
caded. "I shall just have to see what I can do
about that."

"We've more than a year till we're sixteen,
mother," I said.

"I know." Within that sad acknowledgement
was her unspoken knowledge that this war was
not likely to end before the sixteenth anniversary
of our birth. I felt almost guilty that I would wear
my crystal but Tracell, who had shown such
mature fortitude and intelligence, would be
disappointed.

While Mallafret Hall had over twenty bedchambers, it did not have sufficient warm coverings for so many unexpected guests. Even bringing all the horse rugs in from the stable did not suffice and, for the second time in a single day, I saw my mother thwarted in her incredible ability to cope with any crisis, disaster, or problem.

"I shall have to do *something,*" I heard her murmur, clutching her crystals and furiously rubbing them, forcing them to provide an answer.

"Mother, is it possible there're some usable things stored in the presses and trunks in the attics?" All of us children had played up there on rainy days.

"Ooh, milady," Tess said, brightly, "there's ever so many things up there. We had to turn out all the old curtains and things before Lord Emkay left."

Mother's face lit up. She was so delighted that she hugged us both indiscriminately.

"The very things indeed. All those dreary, dreary tapestries that I couldn't bear to throw out! They shall do admirably."

If there was a slight musty smell from being stored so long, no one minded for the heavy brocaded draperies as well as the tapestries were good insulation against the cold. And all, even the rugs that were also discovered in at the apex of roof and rafter, had been carefully wrapped against the moth and provided covering for even the flagstones of the Great Hall. With fires in every hearth, everyone would be able to sleep with more comfort than they would have had even in the snuggest of cottages.

We also discovered carefully preserved garments of long-ago fashions. While some of the gaudy costumes sent people into giggles and smirks, most of the fabrics—having been of the highest quality—remained in good condition. So many of the villagers had fled in their nightclothes from the cannon barrage that they stood in grave need of warmer garments. Best were trunks of liveries and house dresses that had been packed away when Mother had chosen more modern ones. The women and children had a marvelous time sorting out and trying on the apparel.

The sight of Mistress Cooper enveloped in yards of a gauzy material had us all in tears of laughter, especially when she tried to essay a court courtesy and fell flat with an *oof* that also split the back of the dress. She was so distressed that it took Mother nearly half an hour to reassure her. Finally, Mother took a piece of fragile gauze in both hands and, with only the least pressure, split it easily.

"It must be well over a hundred years old, Mistress Cooper. Even the best of fabrics will deteriorate in that long a time."

"A hundred years, milady?" Mistress Cooper's distress was replaced by astonishment.

One chest was stuffed with the voluminous petticoats of the last century which could be turned into night-clothes. Another was full of men's shirts and knee britches. Fortunately many were made of good heavy cloth, and it was decided they could be lengthened against the wintry weather.

"And, I think," Mother said as people departed to their various sleeping chambers, "tomorrow we will see how to alter the old liveries and maids' dresses to fit. Unless there are other calls upon our time and effort."

There were not, though feeding and clothing one hundred and eighty-five home-less people required considerable organization and patience the next day. Mistress Cooper was up almost before Liwy, and the pair wakened four more women to start bread. Liwy did insist on reclaiming her largest cauldron to the kitchen

after its night on the ramparts with oil, no longer
boiling or needed. She remarked on the depth of
the frost on the roofs and had a narrow escape
falling into one of the gutters, but there had to be
sufficient porridge and she would have braved
much worse than mere frost to do her duty as
Mallafret's cook. That report of the bitter cold
worried Mother. Not that the Shupp had ever
frozen solid, since it ran so swiftly. All was snug
inside Mallafret Hall and Mother had to be content that she had accomplished that much.

Stuffed with hot porridge and tightly bundled
with scarves and heavy capes of yesteryear's fashions, Andras and Achill led the older lads out to
bring in more wood to replenish the fires which
had to be kept burning. Even gloves were found
in one wide storage drawer—though they were of
such fine leathers that I saw Mother blanch as she
handed them out—but cold fingers could fumble
and this was no time to try to preserve the anti-
quated when present need was greater. Mind you,
I had to go call the boys in when they were suspi-
ciously long at a task that should been completed
more quickly. At that, Andras and Achill

admitted that they had been the first tempted to skate on the pathways—which were hoarfrosted and made excellent slides.

We spent the rest of the day inspecting the wealth within the trunks and presses under the eaves. Mother did return several of the more magnificent ball gowns to the cambric in which they had been swathed. The formal court wear, stockings, knee britches and such like were also set aside. The rest of the garments—the full sleeved fine cambric and muslin shirts, the long-skirted jerkins and vests, broadcloth jackets which could be dyed more suitable shades than buttercup yellow or pale green, blue, lavender, and gray, and such breeches as there were of the durable fabrics—came out at once.

Every ground floor room became drapers' shops. Garments festooned tables, chairs, fire-screens or waited in orderly piles. Such needles, threads and scissors as we possessed were kept busy until late that night, and it was nothing short of amazing how many people were clad in more modern fashion the next morning.

The intense cold continued. I heard it mur-

mured often that some good had come out of the
bombardment, for never would they have been
so warm and comfortable in the homes they
had lost.

Tray and Keffine returned midmorning for
more supplies. They were red-cheeked and merry
with their new responsibilities, but both had
somehow cleaned up their garments and washed
their faces. Keffine was mounted on a sturdy
well-bred cob while Tray still rode the pony. Old
as the venerable fellow was he too seemed to find
his new occupation to his liking for he pranced
and danced on his hindquarters as much as the
cob did.

"We've some good news for the cottagers,
Mother," Tray said, once again putting down his
feet and letting the pony walk out from under
him. Keffine's merry glance caught mine and I
coughed into my hand rather than laugh outright.
"You may laugh, Tirza," my brother said with
such sublime arrogance that Mother and I both
dissolved into gales of laughter.

"Thank you," I said, when I had quite
exhausted myself with hilarity. "Bread's baked

and some pies are ready and will only need to be reheated," I said, retreating into the house to assemble the victuals.

It was when I returned with my helpers, dressed in their new finery, that Tracell and Keffine Hyland gawked with surprise.

"Have you a troop of mummers, too?" Tray asked, though he accepted the baskets of food readily enough. In fact, he had the pony so laden that there was no room left for him to sit on the sturdy back. Keffine, likewise, dismounted because it was far more important that the food reach the hungry recipients than that he rode comfortably.

I glanced at our unusually clad assistants. "We have been able to do what we could to clothe them all decently," I replied, "by turning out all those old trunks in the attic."

"What a splendid idea," Tray agreed, winking at me for the times we had played with the contents of those self-same discards. "Some came in little more than their shifts, shawls and clogs on their feet."

"Save some shirts and vests for us, would

you?" Tray said, regarding his torn and battered raiment.

"You might tell the villagers that we have found quite a few things that survived the fires," Keffine said. He had the merriest blue eyes.

"Which is why you both look as if you'd been sifting through ash and dirt. Well done, well done," my mother said.

"One way of keeping warm," Tray remarked diffidently.

"But kindly thought of," Mother said.

"There's more usable than we'd've thought," Keffine said, accepting the basket of breads. "Though we did have a spot of trouble when an Effestrian patrol ventured to the river bank and tried to interrupt our labors. We sent them off with such a rain of arrows, they fell over themselves running away."

"More slipping and sliding down the bank," Tray added, grinning.

Mistress Cooper and Mistress Chandler arrived just then, their arms full of cloaks.

"You will need these," Mother said, draping a cloak across Tray's shoulders.

Astonished, he held a fold up, almost sputtering with indignation. "Why, this has to have been last worn by great-great uncle ..."

"Never you mind who wore it last, Viscount Mallafret," my mother said firmly. "It will doubtless deflect arrows as well as keep you warm."

Keffine Hyland bent his knees to allow Mistress Cooper to bestow one on his broad shoulders. He looked quite elegant.

The rest of the warm garments were carefully draped across cob and pony.

"They are indeed welcome, milady," Keffine said, bowing gratefully.

"And these will undoubtedly be as welcome while they hold together." Mother passed each a pair of heavy mailed gauntlets, so ancient that the cloaks were almost modern in comparison.

"Now, these are more suitable for warriors like us," Tray said, stuffing the gloved fingers as far down as he could force them. Then they made their way, proud and tall, down the avenue, leading the laden animals. I wasn't certain in my mind who looked more elegant, my brother or Keffine.

The bitter cold lasted a full week, so that Andras, Achill and some of the sturdier lads had to take cross saws and axes into the home woods to keep us supplied with firing. Under Mother's command, we took the oxen and the heaviest wain left in the village tithe-barn and brought back more wheat which had to be hand-

ground, as the millwheel was frozen solid in the
weir. Several of the men came back from the village and, with our gamekeeper and Tray to guide
them, brought back deer and cleared the snares
of whatever had been trapped and frozen to
death.

While the worst of the cold held, we did not
fear renewed attacks from the Effestrians, and
Lord Monteros sent messengers to Mother, and
from us to Princestown, that he had reinforced
the river banks of his province to prevent enemy
incursions. The returning courier brought very
welcome letters from all our brave soldiers so we
spent Solstice in a merriment that was far from
the doleful occasion it might have been.

Not as bitter but still cold, the winter remained. On such fair days as there were, new
dwellings began to rise in the village, replacing
those burned to the ground. As Tray had said,
iron pots and pans, skillets, even some crockery
had survived the fire. And the chimneys.

Mallafret, in its turn, provided occupation for
all to replace what was lost. Mother turned
everything out of the attic spaces: chests, presses,

tables (that might lack a leg or a brace), chairs that needed re-rushing or re-gluing. She organized those handy with tools to make up additional stools or tables and arranged for the skilled carpenters to replace the lost dower chests. Mallafret was a hive of activity.

Rather than lose valuable space by setting up the big looms, Mother devised a clever and easier method of replacing bedding. In the course of refitting old-fashioned clothing to modern bodies, many pieces and hems and oddments had been cut off. These Mother gave to the youngest and oldest women to piece together into wide bed spreads. Then she had some of this year's wool crop carded fine and stitched in place on one side, while a backing was firmly stitched to provide a triple thickness. Some of the defter needlewomen, having finished redesigning clothing, made interesting patterns of the available colors so that some of the patchwork was quite beautiful as well as warm. All were delighted with the illustrious future use of what might have been discarded as rags.

Spring was late in coming that year, as if even the weather was at war with us. Fair days found everyone who could do anything, even if only holding a ladder steady, helping to rebuild the cottages. The fields were too wet or still too deeply frozen to be ploughed. Everyone worried about planting and so complained to Mother.

"Well, I shall just have to see what can be

done," Mother said and, putting on her oldest boots, mounted Courier, whose stately walk was slow. The best that Tray could say about him was that he eventually got where he was going. And he was very comfortable to ride.

Several times on Mother's tour, he became mired down and had to be hauled out of the mud. Mother spent several days out, going from farm to farm. Pausing in the village on her way, she noted the rise of new habitations. That cheered her, I know, because to have so many people about us constantly in Mallafret had lost any charm. The earlier comradeship in disaster had altered to squabbles that Mother had to arbitrate time and again, taking her away from more urgent planning.

After her inspection tour, she called all together: farmer and villager.

"Where there is too much water, we must dig little channels for it to run to the edges of the fields. Perhaps even line some depressions with stones to preserve the water should we need it in the summer. If this winter has been so wet, we may very well have a very dry summer."

So sensible was the suggestion that despite the very hard work to implement her scheme, it was accomplished. If not all of a field could be ploughed, enough was drained so that seed would not rot. Once such planting was done, work turned back to rebuilding the cottages. And in this regard, Mother had a great deal to say to improve the interiors, the major improvement being her insistence that local slate be used for the roofs rather than the traditional thatch. Since Bart the Thatcher's house had also burned, he allowed as how he could accept the change. By raising all the roofs by two feet, there was sufficient loft space under the eaves to provide more sleeping space and, for those on the ground level, considerably more privacy.

The inn was reconstructed next, with kitchens and nooks snug and open before the next storey was completed. There were not yet many travelers but often couriers passed, and they were grateful for a full night's rest. Mother, in grave conversation with Matt the Innkeeper and his wife, decided that, all things considered, it wouldn't be a bad idea to have a large room added to one side of the inn, suitable for village meetings, assemblies, Solstice dances, and any other functions that required a large indoor space.

"It will, of course," my mother said in the mild way she sometimes used to such good effect when trying to get her way, "be grand for our Victory Celebrations."

And so she had all the enthusiastic help such a project required. However, the large room first saw use as an hospice as walking wounded began to make their way to distant homes. They were grateful for the food and shelter at Mallafret Village, and Mother supervised such nursing as their injuries required.

"Those of Mallafret will have snug dwelling houses to come home to, thanks to your efforts, milady," Sir Minshall reminded her, seeing how downcast the injuries had made her who had been so cheerful through all our adversities.

"I'll have to see what I can do," she said, shaking her head and caressing the crystals.

All too soon, my own crystal would be placed on its chain about my neck, but the prospects of having a horse for my twin diminished from unlikely to impossible. We saw horses from far to the south being driven along the main road to Princestown, resupply for the cavalry.

"There's not one of them," Tray said, his scathing tone hiding disappointment, "worth bothering with. They all have four legs, a head and tail and that's the best that can be said."

Mother and I exchanged glances, and she sighed.

"Then it's as well we have no silver or gold to beg for one," Mother replied with a sly glance at him.

"A waste even if we had any!" Tray replied contemptuously. "They're not worth even stealing."

Taking a deep breath, he turned away from us and went off to help Siggie weed the vegetables.

Mother and I exchanged glances: hers nearly as doting as mine since we knew how keenly he was trying to hide an almost palpable frustration.

"I really will have to see what can be done."

"Mother," I said from all the wisdom of my nearly sixteen years, "sometimes even you can't provide the impossible. Besides which, he has set his heart on a Cirgassian, like our Courier...only not wind-broken."

With the slightest of smiles on her face and her long, slender, workworn fingers sliding up and down the dangling crystals, she replied, "It is true that the impossible takes longer, but the improbable is a force to be reckoned with."

The summer brought so little rain that those reservoirs which Mother had had us construct to drain or retain the excess winter water proved to be the salvation of what crops we had been able to nurture. As fortunate was the fact that Prince Sundimin, with our father now one of his most valued generals, was pursuing the war well into Effestrian lands. Our village was asked to send reinforcements of any male who had reached the age of sixteen and those over forty who were still able in body. This reduced our work force further and worried my mother more. For, inexorably, our sixteenth birthday neared and she feared that Tracell would have to answer the next draft. However much we had both longed to be sixteen and considered adult, that status had lost much of its long-desired charm.

Although it was the custom in our land that if a male child becomes adult at sixteen, it was also true that a girl of that age may put up her hair and go to balls and other social occasions. I, who had once dreamed all sorts of enchantments to occur during my first ball, drearily realized that no such festivity was likely. Imagine then my astonishment when Mother, all smiles and gladness, informed us that of course Mallafret Hall would celebrate our birthday with the traditional ball.

"And what, dear Mother, shall we have to wear to a ball?" I asked rather tartly, since Tracell and I were then most practicably attired in the sturdy knee breeches that even women were wearing as more durable apparel for hoeing fields and rebuilding cottages. Even the thought of a ball, however, was able to reawaken yearnings, which I had so firmly excluded from consideration.

"Why, my dears," and Mother's smile was so mischievous that I found myself smiling back, "we will have our choice of what we want to wear to a ball. A costume ball. You can't have forgotten all the lovely gowns, long coats, embroidered vests, and fine silken breeches which we so admired last winter after the village burned? Who will care if we dress in old-fashioned finery? But dress we will. And Liwy says there will be enough eggs and flour and sweetening to provide a proper birthday cake and other confections to make it the occasion all that it should be. Your father put down wines at your births and these need only to be brought up from the cellar."

"But—but—" Even Tracell was now so accustomed to mundane substitutes that the thought of such extravagance startled him. Or maybe it was the thought of his long-desired and unattainable birthday horse!

"We may be short of many things, my dear Tray, but there are certain times when ceremony must be celebrated. And you both," she encircled our waists with her arms, "deserve whatever we can contrive. And I know exactly what I can do."

"Well, I can't say that you don't contrive minor miracles regularly, Mother," Tray said, admiringly. "But must I wear knee breeches?"

"Indeed you must, my love," she said, unde-terred by his protest, "for you've as fine a leg as your father."

Hands raised in passionate rebellion, Tray took a deep breath.

"Not another word," my mother said, putting her fingers on his mouth. "You'll be surprised at how courtly you will appear. Every girl in the county will be eager to dance with you."

"No powder in my hair..." Tray said, wag-gling a finger under her nose.

"With such lovely titian locks as you have, of course not," Mother said, pretending outrage at the mere suggestion.

"And how are you going to get everyone else to dress up that way?" Tray demanded. I knew he did not wish to dress in uncommon fashion.

"We have not been the only family in the county to have seen what our ancestors put up in their attics," was Mother's blithe reply. "I think the pale green for you, Tracell, so I will allow some of the others to be loaned where they will fit."

By the time he had been forced to try on the

pale green, with its heavy embroidery of silver and froth of lace (bleached to its original white and mildly starched), he spent quite a while observing himself in Mother's triple mirror. Shoes, with buckles and green heels, had also been found and fitted well enough.

"So gallant, milord," Mother said, and we both sank into court curtsies that sent him into guffaws since we were still in our everyday breeches. (They were just a little ludicrous since they were much too long for us and reached our ankles.)

But the prospect had put him in a very good mood. Which, I think, was what Mother had in mind.

The entire village joined to help Mallafret Hall produce an evening that would be memorable. If the journals of our ancestors—which took up several shelves in the library—annotated in precise detail the lavish decorations and extravagant excesses of previous sixteenth birthdays, Mother decreed yet another sensible innovation. This Ball would start early enough in the evening so that the summer length of daylight would not require the use of the thousands of expensive and totally unobtainable tapers to fill the chandeliers and light the proceedings. Indeed, the dancing would be on the greensward below the terrace on the South Face of Mallafret Hall. The lawn, or so Andras and Achill vehemently declared, had been rolled and rolled and all but manicured with embroidery scissors to a level that would be as smooth a surface for dancing as any parquet floor. Garlands of honeysuckle from the hedgerows, gathered by the villagers, draped across the terrace balustrade and wherever such floral decorations were needed. Everyone seemed determined to make this a truly momentous occasion. We were not even daunted by the sultry weather that augured of possible thundershowers. Indeed, from time to time, I could have sworn I heard distant thunder in the east. If that were the case, since our weather went from west to east, our evening would not be spoiled.

Barbecue pits were dug for the several oxen (who might be tough to eat due to their extreme age, but they wouldn't have survived another winter anyway). Many braces of pheasant, grouse, chicken, pigeon, dove, and goose were turning on spits. Carp, tench, and the other fish that had been taken by diligent anglers from local streams were ready to be grilled. The odors of roasting meats and game encouraged us to work the harder to make all ready for the party.

"We all deserve it," Diana said, and Desma, much as I had been the silent second to my brother's remarks, nodded emphatically.

"Now you must sit still," Catron told them, for we had dressed them first since our toilettes would take longer. As a special concession to keep them occupied, they were allowed to watch us dress, Catron giggling nearly as much as I, as we struggled into the corselettes and hoops and petticoats required to underpin our lovely gowns. And then they took turns pulling the corset strings in so tight I was afraid I'd never be able to dance, much less eat of our birthday feast.

Mother had designated the pale yellow gown which had been so admired the previous winter for Catron, since it suited not only her fourteen years but her dark hair and fair skin. As Catron was taller than whomever the dress had been created for, it reached the middle of her lower limbs, the perfect length for her. Since I was now a few hours short of being officially sixteen, I was allowed to wear a much more elaborate and delectable confection of white gauze over silver silk. Throwing a muslin cape over Catron's shoulders, Mother first braided my sister's dark locks tightly to a point just below the nape of her neck. Then she allowed the lovely natural curls to fall to Catron's waist: still a young style but with just enough fashion to please my sister.

My dark red hair was piled and pinned atop my hair, save for the three long ringlets which, with her curling iron, Mother created to fall from the back knot of my hair across my shoulder to hang nearly to the decolletage of the low cut gown.

Then she placed on both our heads, as if tiaras of priceless gems, headbands of honeysuckle and daisies. Catron and I exclaimed and twirled and whirled in front of the mirror while our younger sisters were struck dumb at the change in us.

"These should be roses or something more exotic," Mother said apologetically as she arranged garlands. "Now, for just one more detail," she said and left the room.

We were both fidgeting at what seemed a very long delay—we were so eager to show everyone else how fine we looked—when she returned with two flat black velvet cases: one round, one long.

"Pearls are suitable for you, Catron," she said and opened the first of the cases to remove the strand of pink-toned pearls that fit around Catron's lovely neck as if they had been strung for her alone. "Now, you may take your sisters downstairs and you are *all,*" and Mother held up a stern finger, "to sit quietly in the hall where you may move *only* to welcome early-come guests should some arrive before Tracell, Tirza, and I descend."

An ecstatic Catron let go of her pearls to take her sisters' hands and leave the room. Then, with an air of ceremony, Mother turned to me, the long case in her hand.

"You are not precisely sixteen, dearest Tirza, but you have acted with such wisdom in the last

trying years that I feel I am conforming to tradition in letting you choose your crystal today, on
the eve of your sixteenth birthday."

I almost burst into tears. "But what shall we
do about Tray and his horse, mother?"

Tears were in her eyes as she embraced me.

"You make my heart leap with pride, my darling. Not that I haven't cudgeled my brains in an
effort to make his birthday wish come true,
but..." and she gave a little sigh, half-sob, half a
catch of her breath. Brisk again, she opened the
case to show me the four crystals nestled there,
each on fine linked chains similar to those she
wore: one crystal for each of her daughters. "I
will tell you—when we have more time—how to
understand the use of these crystals. You will find
that that their main purpose is an aid to help you
focus your mind on what needs to be done. I
believe yours will help you refine instincts that I
have already seen you exhibit."

I didn't really absorb her words, for the sight
of beautiful jewels awed me. I fancied I heard
gentle music, the kind heard when delicate crystal
is lightly pinged by a finger. No two of the crys-

tals in that box were alike. One, two finger-joints long, was the palest of blues, its facets cut cleanly and ending in a point. Another, slightly shorter, blushed the pink of the most delicate rose. The third was the dainty yellow-green of the peridot.

"That's Catron's," I blurted out.

Mother chuckled. "You may well be right, my love."

It was the fourth, the clear one, not white but seeming to hold all the rainbow colors when the sun coming through the window touched it briefly. It was the one to which my hand instinctively went. I saw out of the corner of my eye that Mother nodded once, as if she had known this would be my choice.

"This was the one you reached for when you were barely three months old and my mother and grandmother brought crystals to see which would suit you best."

"That long ago?"

"As the world turns, it is not *that* long ago, love."

She put it around my neck and embraced me with a kiss on each cheek and one on my lips. As soon as the crystal settled against the skin of my chest, I could feel the warmth of it.

"Oh!" I was surprised.

"Oh?" Mother echoed, her eyebrows rising in query.

"It's warm. I thought a crystal would be cool."

My mother gave me a long and searching look. "That depends on the crystal, but obviously your choice is well made and the crystal is content to be worn by you." We were both startled by the sound of thunder. "It seems the heavens agree with me. When we have more time, I will explain some of the properties of these particular crystals and how the women of our line have learned to depend on them."

"Do they," and I pointed to the three she wore—this time looped onto a black velvet band at her throat so that each, the tender-blue, then the white and the deep green—dangled separately, "tell you what to do all the time, Mother?"

She laughed. "Not in so many words, love, but they do help focus the mind when sensible thought is required. Generally they take some heat from our bodies. If it should ever get very hot or very cold, come to me instantly. Now," and she turned brisk, "you must help me dress, for if I do not mistake the sounds, some of our guests are arriving."

Indeed, the rumbling thunder to the east had caused many of our invited guests to hurry, lest they in their finery be caught in a sudden shower. Mind you, the manner of transport which brought many of them started the party in high good humor. So few horses remained in the county that other animals had been substituted. Several carts were drawn by not so willing pairs of goats. One elegant barouche was stately drawn by two sets of yoked oxen, while four mismatched mules pulled a landau. More than one conveyance used donkeys, hee-hawing up the drive as if commenting on their new occupation so that all would notice their promotion. Several farmers actually pushed their elegantly dressed wives in barrows so their dainty fabrics would not be soiled by road dust. Those from the village were perhaps grateful that they did not have far to walk. I did see some reach the gates and pause to dust their feet before putting on their dancing slippers.

Of course, Mother had been very generous with the contents of our attic. We did recognize some of the fine gowns and male attire. And if the fashions were of different centuries, we were all most elegantly costumed. Tracell had never looked so handsome, nor so like Father, as he did in the pale green wide-skirted long jacket, with the beautifully embroidered paler green waist-coat and white silk knee breeches. I felt that Keffine was as handsome in the blue, and his father, Lord Hyland, posed as a remarkable figure in his purple. Lady Hyland was certainly flattered by the lavender silk with its gauzy over-skirt trimmed with silver lace. There had not been enough of the old-fashioned apparel to fit or costume everyone of rank in the county from our stores, but following our example, many appeared in what they had been able to discover. The gentlemen attired themselves, if informally, in fine cambric white full sleeved shirts, worn with elegant lacy froths at the throat, long vests, and tight court pants. Women appeared in every sort of bodices, full skirts, and embroidered or lacy aprons every bit as elegant as their menfolk. As well we were out of doors, for many had preserved their garments from the moth by camphor, which airing had not completely removed and which the heat of the afternoon made more redolent.

Old liveries had been unearthed and freshened so that those who served the gathering did so as stylishly as those they waited upon. I don't know who found the outfits for the village musicians, but they were certainly clad for a grand occasion and seemed indefatigable in their energetic playing of old galliards, gavottes, reels, set dances, and minuets. Their tankards were rarely left unreplenished. Perhaps the food did not rival the victuals or fancies that had been served at other such Balls, but there was sufficient for all to partake until the roasts were finished. Portions of the fish and fowl were passed around, with napkins, and with fine wine or beer or cider to wash these tidbits down, so the dancing took on an exuberance that equaled the occasion.

By tradition, the birthday child or children

danced first. It should have been my father who bowed to ask for my hand, but Tracell did the honors for me. And to accept his hand I had to release my beautiful, exciting crystal for the first time since Mother had put it on my neck. Maybe, just maybe, my fervent prayers for him would be answered, though I had not had been able to focus my mind on any manner in which I could spring a horse out of nowhere for Tray. Then Tray, again assuming my father's traditional role, swirled Mother, ravishing in the deep red that was so close a match to her glorious hair, onto the floor while the spectators cheered.

Keffine was next to ask my hand for a dance, and I only too delighted to accede as Tray partnered an ecstatic Catron. As my white and silver skirts whirled against Keffine's blue coat, I felt we made as handsome a couple as Mother and Tray. Keffine had to relinquish my hand to his father who, while no longer as agile as his son, had obviously instructed Keffine in all manner of dances. Protocol now properly observed, others took the floor.

During the short intervals, we were aware of

more thunder, but no one was going to permit mere weather to interrupt this party. Who knew when the young men asking to dance with me or Catron (since Mother permitted her to stand up for the reels and sets) or those of the other pretty girls of our neighborhood would spend their next days? So many were now eligible to answer any new muster that the prince might call. I won't say that the atmosphere had even a touch of frenzy or premonition, though my crystal continued to feel comfortably warm against my skin, but this evening was for our enjoyment. And we were all determined to forget such things as the war and the sparse harvest that must see us through another long winter with so many other items in scarce supply.

We were indeed so single-minded in our enjoyment of the pleasures of the occasion that it wasn't until the horse walked out onto the terrace that we were forced to recall what we had managed to place at the back of our minds.

It was Andras who caught up the one remaining rein, and only half of it at that. The horse was so weary that it was possibly as happy to be standing still. My first thought was that it was a Cirgassian, though nowhere near as exhausted as Courier had been on his arrival at Mallafret. The fiddlers stopped, bows scraping dissonantly, the flute piping awkwardly into silence and the accordion ending on a dissonance from lack of air. We all turned and stared.

This horse could not be the answer to *my* prayers, for on closer inspection we saw that dried blood and lather coated the creature. Its saddle was askew and the dark stain smeared on the seat could only be more dried blood. No stirrups remained, nor a saber scabbard nor saddle-bags.

Both Tray and Keffine approached the horse carefully, for the animal was in distress, its sides heaving. Tray caught a bun from the nearest plate, which he held out to the animal. It sniffed, extending its neck, snatched the bun, and devoured it. At a gesture from Tray, Andras and Achill immediately filled their hands with bread to bring to Keffine and him. In that sudden silence, we were all aware that the thunder we had attributed to the weather had not been caused by that phenomenon, and fear spread as rapidly as if it had the night of the first bombardment we had suffered.

Because we were at the back of the house, on the greensward, with music enthusiastically played, the noise to the east had been muffled. Hand on my crystal, which was neither hot nor cold but as warm as my skin, I turned to Mother. She had her hand spread over the three at her neck and gave the littlest shake of her head.

"We had best investigate," Lord Hyland said and glanced hopefully at the horse.

"He's wounded, Lord Hyland," Tray said, pointing out the clotted blood down his near side, discoloring the white fetlock.

"The saddle's wet, Tray," Keffine said, "and with water. He's been swimming." As the horse continued to munch the food offered him, Keffine carefully loosed the girth of the off-center saddle and removed it from the horse's back. The badly placed saddle had rubbed raw patches.

Achill had the presence of mind to find a basin and fill it with water, which the horse sucked eagerly.

"Milord." One of the farmers came up to Lord Hyland with a big sturdy mule. "It's not at all what I'd offer in better times…"

"Ooh, not in those britches, milord," Lady Hyland exclaimed, appalled to see such splendor ruined in a saddle.

"Keffine, see what else there is to ride," Lord Hyland said and, disregarding his wife's continued reproaches, mounted the mule.

"I'll come, too," Tracell said, and encouraging the horse to follow, beckoned for his brothers to accompany him.

Donkeys were gathered from the paddocks in which they had been tethered. Mother and other ladies brought out the muskets, long rifles and such other weapons as might be useful, handing them around to the quickly assembled reconnoitering force. Then Tray trotted out from the stable yard on his pony, feet stuck out in his fine shoes so as not to be dragged on the ground. He had discarded his elegant coat and vest and somehow found a more practical pair of ancient trousers, which he had secured with a stirrup leather about his slim waist. Keffine, down to shirtsleeves and an equally disreputable pair of breeches, bestrode a donkey not much larger than Tray's venerable pony.

So variously mounted, the men sallied forth. Lord Hyland, on the much larger mule, led the way, equipped with the saber and pistols my mother had supplied.

Those who could not find four legs to use—no one attempted any of the goats—used their own two to follow Lord Hyland, leaving the rest of us in the midst of the party splendor.

I took such comfort as I could from the fact that my lovely crystal remained merely warm. I saw Mother's fingers alternating between her three and moved to her side. Once the men had gone, we women and children seemed directionless, all joy in our festivities abandoned.

"Well, we certainly cannot allow the roasts to burn," Mother said, taking charge again. "Mistress Cooper, will you not tend one, and Mistress Chandler, the other. Tirza love, gather up the aprons our chefs discarded. I for one do not care to ruin my finery. Liwy, Catron, and Tess can see to the spits with whoever is willing to help turn them. We cannot waste good food, and doubtless the men will be hungry when they return."

"Shouldn't we change, Mother?" I asked.

My mother smiled. "No," she said slowly. "We must allow you as much of your birthday as possible."

"I've *had* my birthday, Mother," I said, for the first time contesting her.

That caused everyone to stop and stare at me and, for one moment, I could have sunk in the ground with dismay at my impudence.

"Thunder's gone," Mistress Cooper announced into the silence that lengthened as we all listened as hard as we could.

"It could have *been* thunder," Mistress Chandler offered.

"That horse was wounded," Lady Hyland said sternly. "With saber cuts. And he had swum the river. Clearly he escaped from some sort of a battle."

"The men will send a messenger as soon as may be to reassure us. And do they all or only some return, there will be edible food to sustain them. So please turn that ox before it becomes charcoal, Mistress Chandler." My mother spun one finger to remind the woman of her duty.

That was when three more horses were seen, grazing as if they had seen nary a blade of green grass for weeks. Two had no saddles and only torn remnants of bridles; the third was so badly scored on flank and withers that it was obvious the animal had followed its picket mates out of habit. They offered no resistance at all when we tried to lure them into the stable yard, where Siggie and those lads too young to be allowed to accompany the scouting party were able to attend them.

Mother found some sort of a driving coat, wearing it back to front, to cover her red dress because the most badly injured animal would need to have the terrible gash along his flank stitched or he would die from blood loss. I found a similar garment—one of father's I think—to protect my ball gown so I could sew up the gashes on the first animal, although Siggie had to use a twitch to keep him still enough for me to set the stitches. There were many willing helpers to wash and spread honey on the nicks and smaller cuts and generally see to the comfort of our four war refugees.

By the time we had finished those, just as Mother and I were about to doff the thick and confining garments, more horses stumbled in ... Cirgassians from their small pointed ears and conformation.

"My darling Tirza," Mother said to me, bemused as we watched a veritable troop of wet and tired animals limping into the yard—for horses will smell the presence of other equines as well as food. "I know how close you are to your twin, but surely you should have realized that *I* was going to make sure of some sort of a birthday horse for him?"

"Yes, but I wanted to make *certain sure,* Mother." My hand went to my crystal and I snatched it away, blowing on my fingers.

Mother, seeing that, reached for hers and, with equal alacrity, let them go.

"What is it, mother?" I cried fearfully.

"Off with that garment," and she was stripping hers, spreading her skirts out again from the confinement. "My hair? Is it mussed?"

"No, but our hands—"

While we had washed before tending the animals, we had not yet removed the traces of our ministrations.

Leaning over the horse trough in the stable yard without touching her dress to its wet sides, mother scrubbed her hands and arms as quickly as she could, gesturing for me to do so. We also heard shouting that added haste to our ablutions. She did pause long enough to be sure there was nothing under her fingernails, and I did the same. The cheers and shouts were jubilant, coming from the front of the Hall.

Mother picked up her skirts and ran, skipping around the droppings which no one had had time to sweep up from the usually spotless cobbles. I followed, also trying to straighten the edges of my overskirt that had been crushed down under the protective clothing I had worn. We also had to wend our way past even more horses that had run away from whatever battle they had ridden into.

We took the side gate out of the former rose garden that had supplied us with vegetables the past two years and down the pebbled side of Mallafret. Mother's upraised arm stopped my helter-skelter progress, for the wide driveway was full of horses, mules, men, and weeping women embracing haggard but happy soldiery. Lord Hyland sat his mule with great dignity and, seeing our arrival, pointed and shouted.

"Here they are, milord!"

Out of the press a horse was urged forward, and Mother, uttering a cry of great joy, ran in that direction. I started to follow but halted, taking in what she evidently ignored or, in relief at the sight of his tall figure, did not see: bandages and a tunic that showed tears and holes. My eyes fixed on the left hand, reaching for her, and the bandage that looked far too narrow to be covering four fingers. An even older, dirtier wrapping covered the left side of his head, half hidden under a military cap set at a jaunty angle as if to hide as much of the bandage as possible. But even as she reached him, she touched first his left hand and then his forehead. Then allowed herself to be swung up in his arms and twirled around.

I could see her speaking to him and knew, without any sound, what she must be saying: "I must see what I can do about these."

Then Father threw back his head, laughing. "Why else do you think I have returned to you?" he said with such a jubilant tone that I knew he had not been as badly injured as he appeared. He whirled her again and, though one cheek was pressed against hers, I could see him wince. Well, he was home and Mother would certainly see what she could do about healing him.

From the fragments of joyful welcome around me, I knew that the war was over, that the thunder we had heard had come from Prince Sundimin's artillery, sending the Effestrians running for whatever safety they could find. Even their most recent allies, the plains' Cirgassians whose brave horses had taken refuge at Mallafret Hall, were in full retreat...many of them no doubt reduced to walking.

Father had been ordered south along the Shupp to intercept whatever stragglers came ashore to terrorize our people or seek merciful sanctuary from that final rout. (Not many that attempted the river survived.) The Shupp might not have been an insurmountable obstacle for horses bred to cross the swift and dangerous mountain rivers of the Cirgassian homelands, but only the strongest of human swimmers could have breasted those treacherous currents and come ashore. We learned later that many of the Cirgassian horses that managed to stagger up our banks had been swept miles down from their point of entry on the final battleground.

Then Father strode towards me, and I nearly sobbed to see the twinkling in his eyes, the way they crinkled with his happiness, and the proud expression on his dirty tired face: pride of me, his daughter.

"I did mean to be here at your sixteenth, daughter dear, but that is surely tomorrow unless I have somehow lost a day in that fearsome battle we won."

"We were informed that there would be another muster, my love," Mother said, one arm about his waist, heedless of the mud, dust, and other stains now rubbing against her beautiful gown, so glad was she to be holding him again, "so it seemed a sensible idea to celebrate the day before should he be required to answer his prince's call."

"So you decided on a costume ball?"

"Indeed, my dear lord," Mother said, laughingly dismissing the past years of hardship and scarcities, "a costume ball was the very thing. And indeed the only festive apparel most of us had to our backs." She gestured to the guests, mingling now with restored husbands, fathers, and sons. "And the early hour makes it unnecessary to use tapers, which we don't have anyway."

"We could not have had a more glorious welcome home had we sent out invitations, my love. How marvelous it is to see elegant women in beautiful gowns!" Then he leaned forward to touch the crystal at my throat. "As I recall, it is the very one your baby hands reached for." He kissed my forehead and then each cheek. "So where is my birthday son?" he now

demanded, wheeling Mother around to search
for Tracell in the throng. "What finery did he
assume for this prenatal celebration? I have
brought him something which I believed he
greatly desired and which, indeed, I had
promised to provide."

He pointed then to where his war-horse stood,
single-mindedly cropping grass. That was when
we realized his equerry held the reins of two
grazing horses and was being pulled first in one
direction and then the other. The unsaddled
animal was nearly as tall as Father's and so dark
a shade he gleamed bluely in the now fading
evening light.

"Tracell is in a very elegant shade of green...."
Mother began and then pointed down the
avenue.

"Great heavens ..." my father exclaimed, so
stunned at the sight that he slapped his right hand
to his forehead. For Tray, legs straight out before
him, was galloping the pony across the lawn, the
nimble little beast weaving his way among the
assembled.

Father, roaring with laughter at the approaching vision, doubled up with mirth as Tray dropped his legs to the ground and let the pony run out from under him. "That will never do for the son of the General Lord Eircelly."

"I was setting sentries along the Shupp, Father, before your sergeant arrived to take over their disposition and informed me of your turn," Tray said, standing just short of father, unsure whether to bow or salute. Father took the initiative and embraced his son—the two were nearly of a height so much had Tracell grown in the last two years. As men will, they were thumping each other on the back until both Mother and I saw that Tracell's young strength had too much force for a man who was certainly not recovered from his wounds.

Tracell caught mother's gesture and stepped back from Father, a trifle embarrassed at how warm a greeting he had given a nation's hero.

"Bring the Cirgassian over here, Barton," my father called to his equerry. "My old fellow knows he's home and will not wander." So Barton, wrapping the charger's reins safely around his neck, trotted over with the fine young animal. "One of my spoils, Tray, when we took an entire remount contingent by surprise. I knew he would suit you. Rising three and entire. I doubt his like will be matched anywhere." Father beamed with pride as Tracell, his eyes gleaming with delight as he circled the proud horse who stood, head high, as if he knew he was being closely inspected. "Prince Sundimin himself approved my choice when he learned the reason for the gift."

Just then Andras, Achill, and two of their peers came charging through the stable gate.

"There're ever so many more wandering in, Tray, that Siggie doesn't know where to put them...*Father!*"

The Cirgassian plunged in alarm at their ecstatic race to Father, and the two boys all but climbed him in their efforts to kiss and hug him joyfully. They had, indeed, been so busy succoring the tired and injured strays that they had not realized what had happened at the front of the Hall.

"Well, let us just see what other jetsam has landed in our demesne," my Father said, setting the boys down again and letting himself be pulled towards the stable yard. He looked back to see that Tracell had calmed the excitable young horse and was leading him towards a quieter section of our crowded front lawn.

"My dear Talarrie," my father exclaimed as he paused to behold the stable yard so full of horses there seemed little space for the grooms attempting to feed and water them, "could it be that you have overworked your crystals?"

"I asked only for one," she said and pointedly did not glance in my direction, though I, too, had only asked for one. "But since we must replace horses for all our tenants and neighbors, perhaps that accounts for these numbers."

"You have always been the most generous of..." He broke off, stiffening, his head unerringly turning towards greensward where the delectable aromas of roasting meats quite overwhelmed the odors which can occur in any stable yard. "Is it at all possible that there might be something left of this early birthday feast?" he asked, his face wistfully hopeful.

She patted his hand and turned him in the right direction where I knew that our festivities would recommence with true joy and celebration.

"I'll see what we can do!"

As it was then, so it is now.

The End

For those who love the
Carpathian novels of Christine Feehan,
here is a preview of a sweeping tale of
encroaching darkness and healing
light by an exciting new author.

C. L. WILSON

*Lord of the
Fading Lands*

PROLOGUE

Loudly, proudly, tairen sing,
As they soar on mighty wings
Softly, sadly, mothers cry
To sing a tairen's lullabye.
—The Tairen's Lament, Fey Nursery Rhyme

The tairen were dying.

Rain Tairen Soul, king of the Fey, could no longer deny the truth. Nor, despite all his vast power and centuries of trying, could he figure a way to save either the creatures that were his soul-kin or the people who depended upon him to lead and defend them.

The tairen—those magnificent, magical, winged cats of the Fading Lands—had only one fertile female left in their pride, and she grew weaker by the day as she fed her strength to her six unhatched kitlings. With those tiny, unborn lives rested the last hope of a future for the tairen, and the last hope of a future for Rain's people, the Fey. But today, the painful truth had become clear. The mysterious, deadly wasting disease that had decimated the tairen over the last millennium had sunk its evil, invisible claws into yet another clutch of unhatched kits.

When the tairen died, so too would the Fey. The fates of the two species were forever intertwined, and had been since the misty time before memory.

Rain looked around the wide, empty expanse of the Hall of Tairen. Indeed, he thought grimly, the death of the immortal Fey had begun centuries ago.

Once, in a time he could still remember, the Hall had rung with the sound of hundreds of Fey Lords, warriors, *shei'dalins* and Tairen Souls arguing politics and debating treaties. Those days had long passed. The Hall was silent now, as silent as the long-abandoned cities of the Fey, as silent as Fey nurseries, as silent as the graves of all those Fey who had died in the Mage Wars a thousand years ago.

Now the last hope for both the tairen and the Fey was dying, and Rain sensed a growing darkness in the east, in the land of his ancient enemies, the Mages of Eld. He couldn't help believing the two events were somehow connected.

He turned to face the huge priceless globe of magical Tairen's Eye crystal called the Eye of Truth, which occupied the center of the room. Displayed on the wings of a man-high stand fashioned from three golden tairen, the Eye was an oracle in which a trained seer could search for answers in the past, the present, and the infinite possibilities of the future. The globe was ominously dark and murky now, the future a dim, forbidding shadow. If there was a way to halt the relentless extermination of his peoples, the answer lay there, within the Eye.

The Eye of Truth had been guarding its secrets, showing shadows but no clear visions. It had resisted the probes of even the most talented of the Fey's still living seers, played coy with even their most beguiling of magic weaves. The Eye was, after all, tairen-made. By its very nature, it combined pride with cunning, passion with often-wicked playfulness. Seers approached it with respect, humbly asked it for a viewing, courted its favor with their minds and their magic but never their touch.

The Eye of Truth was never to be touched.

It was a golden rule of childhood, drummed into the head of every Fey from infant to ancient.

The Eye held the concentrated magic of ages, power so pure and undiluted that laying hands upon the Eye would be like laying hands upon the Great Sun.

But the Eye was keeping secrets, and Rain Tairen Soul was a desperate king with no time to waste and no patience for protocol. The Eye of Truth *would* be touched. He was the king, and he would have his answers. He would wrest them from the oracle by force, if necessary.

His hands rose. He summoned power effortlessly and wove it with consummate skill. Silvery white Air formed magical webs that he laid upon the doors, walls, floor, and ceiling. A spidery network of lavender Spirit joined the Air, then Earth to seal all entrances to the Hall. None would enter to disturb him. No scream, no whisper, no mental cry could pass those shields. Come good or ill, he would wrest his answers from the Eye without interruption—and if it demanded a life for his impertinence, it would be unable to claim any but his.

He closed his eyes and cleared his mind of every thought not centered on his current purpose. His breathing became deep and even, going in and out of his lungs in a slow rhythm that kept time with the beat of his heart. His entire being contracted into a single shining blade of determination.

His eyes flashed open, and Rain Tairen Soul reached out both hands to grasp the Eye of Truth.

"Aaahh!" Power—immeasurable, immutable—arced through him. His head was flung back beneath its onslaught, his teeth bared, his throat straining with a scream of agony. Pain drilled his body like a thousand *sel'dor* blades, and despite twelve hundred years of learning to absorb pain, to embrace it and mute it, Rainier writhed in torment.

This pain was unlike any he had ever known.

This pain refused to be contained.

Fire seared his veins and scorched his skin. He felt his soul splinter and his bones melt. The Eye was angry at his daring affront. He had assaulted it with his bare hands and bare power, and such was not to be borne. Its fury screeched along his bones, vibrating down his spine, slashing at every nerve in his body until tears spilled from his eyes and blood dripped from his mouth where he bit his lip to keep from screaming.

"Nei," he gasped. "I am the Tairen Soul, and I will have my answer."

If the Eye wished to cement the extinction of both tairen and Fey, it would claim Rain's life. He was not afraid of death; rather he longed for it.

He surrendered himself to the Eye and forced his tortured body to relax. Power and pain flowed into him, through him, claiming him without resistance. And when the violent rush of power had invaded his every cell, when the pain filled his entire being, a strange calm settled over him. The agony was there, extreme and nearly overwhelming, but without resistance he was able to distance his mind from his body's torture, to disassociate the agony of the physical from the determination of the mental. He forced his lips to move, his voice a hoarse, cracked whisper of sound that spoke ancient words of power to capture the Eye's immense magic in flows of Air, Water, Fire, Earth, and Spirit.

His eyes opened, glowing bright as twin moons in the dark reflection of the Eye, burning like coals in a face bone white with pain.

With voice and mind combined, Rain Tairen Soul asked his question: "How can I save the tairen and the Fey?"

Relentlessly, absorbing the agony of direct contact with the Eye, he searched its raging depths for answers. Millions of possibilities flashed before his eyes, countless variations on possible futures, countless retellings of past events. Millennia passed in an instant, visions so rapid his physical sight could never have hoped to discern them, yet his mind, steadily commanding the threads of magic, absorbed the images and processed them with brutal clarity. He stood witness to the deaths of billions, the rise and fall of entire civilizations. Angry, unfettered magic grew wild in the world and Mages worked their evil deeds. Tairen shrieked in pain, immolating the world in their agony. Fey women wept oceans of tears, and Fey warriors fell helpless to their knees, as weak as infants. Rain's mind screamed to reject the visions, yet still his hands gripped the Eye of Truth, and still he voiced his question, demanding an answer.

"How can I save the tairen and the Fey?"

He saw himself in tairen form, raining death indiscriminately upon unarmed masses, his own tairen claws impaling Fey warriors.

"How can I save the tairen and the Fey?"

Sariel lay bloody and broken at his feet, pierced by hundreds of knives, half her face scorched black by Mage fire. She reached out to him, her burned and bloodied mouth forming his name. He watched in helpless paralysis as the flashing arc of an Elden Mage's black *sel'dor* blade sliced down across her neck. Bright red blood fountained. . . .

The unutterable pain of Sariel's death—tempered by centuries of life without her—surged back to life with soul-shredding rawness. Rage and bloodlust exploded within him, mindless, visceral, unstoppable. It was the Fey Wilding rage, fueled by a tairen's primal fury, unfettered emotions backed by lethal fangs, incinerating fire, and access to unimaginable power.

They would die! They had slain his mate, and they would all die for their crime! His shrieking soul grasped eagerly for the madness, the power to kill without remorse, to scorch the earth and leave nothing but smoldering ruins and death.

"Nei!" Rain yanked his hands from the Eye and flung up his arms to cover his face. His breath came in harsh pants as he battled to control his fury. Once before, in a moment

of madness and unendurable pain, he had unleashed the beast in his soul and rained death upon the world. He had slain thousands in mere moments, laid waste to half a continent within a few bells. It had taken the combined will of every still-living tairen and Fey to cage his madness.

"*Nei!* Please," he begged, clawing for self-possession. He released the weaves connecting him to the Eye in a frantic hope that shearing the tie would stop the rage fighting to claim him.

Instead, it was as if he had called Fire in an oil vault.

The world was suddenly bathed in blood as his vision turned red. The tairen in him shrieked for release. To his horror, he felt his body begin to dissolve, saw the black fur form, the lethal curve of tairen claws spear the air.

For the first time in twelve hundred years of life, Rainier vel'En Daris knew absolute terror.

The magic he'd woven throughout the Hall would never hold a Tairen Soul caught up in a Fey Wilding rage. All would die. The world would die.

The Tairen-Change moved over him in horrible slow motion, creeping up his limbs, taunting him with his inability to stop it. The small sane part of his mind watched like a stunned, helpless spectator, seeing his own death hurtling towards him and realizing with detached horror that he was going to die and there was nothing he could do to prevent it.

He had overestimated his own power and utterly underestimated that of the Eye of Truth.

"Stop," he shouted. "I beg you. Stop! Don't do this." Without pride or shame, he fell to his knees before the ancient oracle.

The rage left him as suddenly as it had come.

In a flash of light, his tairen-form disappeared. Flesh, sinew, and bone reformed into the lean, muscular lines of his Fey body. He collapsed face down on the floor, gasping for breath, the sweat of terror streaming from his pores, his muscles shaking uncontrollably.

Faint laughter whispered across the stone floor and danced on the intricately carved columns that lined either side of the Hall of Tairen.

The Eye mocked him for his arrogance.

"Aiyah," he whispered, his eyes closed. "I deserve it. But I am desperate. Our people—mine and yours both—face extinction. And now dark magic is rising again in Eld. Would you not also have dared any wrath to save our people?"

The laughter faded, and silence fell over the Hall, broken only by the wordless noises coming from Rain himself, the sobbing gasp of his breath, the quiet groans of pain he didn't have the strength to hold back. In the silence, power gathered. The fine hairs on his arms and the back of his neck stood on end. He became aware of light, a kaleidoscope of color bathing the Hall, flickering through the thin veil of his eyelids.

His eyes opened—then went wide with wonder.

There, from its perch atop the wings of three golden tairen, the Eye of Truth shone with resplendent clarity, a crystalline globe blazing with light. Prisms of radiant color beamed out in undulating waves.

Stunned, he struggled to his knees and reached out instinctively towards the Eye. It wasn't until his fingers were close enough to draw tiny stinging arcs of power from the stone that he came to his senses and snatched his hands back without touching the oracle's polished surface.

There had been something in the Eye's radiant depths—an image of what looked like a woman's face—but all he could make out were fading sparkles of lush green surrounded by orange flame. A fine mist formed in the center of the Eye, then slowly cleared as another vision formed. This image he saw clearly as it came into focus, and he recognized it instantly. It was a city he knew well, a city he despised. The second image faded and the Eye dimmed, but it was enough. Rain Tairen Soul had his answer. He knew his path.

With a groan, he rose slowly to his feet. His knees trembled, and he staggered back against the throne to collapse on the cushioned seat.

Rain gazed at the Eye of Truth with newfound respect. He was the Tairen Soul, the most powerful Fey alive, and yet the Eye had reduced him to a weeping infant in mere moments. If it had not decided to release him, it could have used him to destroy the world. Instead, once it had beaten the arrogance out of him, it had given up at least one of the secrets it was hiding.

He reached out to the Eye with a lightly woven stream of Air, Fire and Water and whisked away the faint smudges left behind by the fingers he had dared to place upon it.

«Sieks'ta. Thank you.» He filled his mental tone with genuine respect and was rewarded by the instant muting of his body's pain. With a bow to the Eye of Truth, he strode towards the massive carved wooden doors at the end of the Hall of Tairen and tore down his weaves.

«Marissya.» He sent the call to the Fey's strongest living *shei'dalin* even as he reached out with Air to swing open the Hall's heavy doors before him. The Fey warriors guarding the door to the Hall of Tairen nodded in response to the orders he issued with swift, flashing motions of his hands as he strode by, and the flurry of movement behind him assured him his orders were being carried out.

«Rain?» Marissya's mental voice was as soothing as her physical one, her curiosity mild and patient.

«A change of plans. I'm for Celieria in the morning and I'm doubling your guard. Let your kindred know the Feyreisen is coming with you.»

Even across the city, he could feel her shocked surprise, and it almost made him smile.

Half a continent away, in the mortal city of Celieria, Ellysetta Baristani huddled in the corner of her tiny bedroom room, tears running freely down her face, her body trembling uncontrollably.

The nightmare had been so real, the agony so intense.

Dozens of angry, stinging welts scored her skin . . . self-inflicted claw marks that might have been worse had her fingernails been longer. But worse than the pain of the nightmare had been the helpless rage and the soul-shredding sense of loss, the raw animal fury of a mortally wounded heart. Her own soul had cried out in empathetic sorrow, feeling the tortured emotions as if they had been her own.

And then she'd sensed something else. Something dark and eager and evil. A crouching malevolent presence that had ripped her out of sleep, bringing her bolt upright in her bed, a smothered cry of familiar terror on her lips.

She covered her eyes with shaking hands. *Please, gods, not again.*

CHAPTER ONE

"Ellie, don't be such a soggy *dorn*." Nine-year-old Lorelle Baristani pouted at her older sister.

It was, in Ellysetta's opinion, an adorable pout. Lorelle's out-thrust lower lip was plump and pink, her round cheeks soft as satin, and her big brown eyes heart-tuggingly soulful. The whole enchanting picture was complemented by masses of mink brown ringlets, and more than one seasoned adult had been known to abandon common sense in the face of such considerable infant artillery. Unfortunately for Lorelle, Ellie was made of sterner stuff.

She smiled and bent to kiss her sister's cheek. "A soggy *dorn*, am I? Just because I don't want to spend the whole day caught up in what's sure to be the worst crush in the past year? And for what? To catch a glimpse of a Fey warrior's head as he walks past?" Ellie shook her head and punched down the bread dough she was making for tonight's dinner rolls.

Tomorrow was the much-anticipated annual visit of the *shei'dalin* Marissya v'En Solande. Her arrival was always a spectacle as she and her guard of one hundred fierce leather- and steel-bedecked Fey warriors entered the city and marched down the main thoroughfare to the palace.

A week ago, Ellysetta would have gone, no matter how long the wait, just for the chance of glimpsing the glint off a Fey blade. But that was before her disturbing nightmare and before the dark dreams that had continued to haunt her ever since. When she woke each morning, her skin felt tight, her muscles inexplicably sore and weary, as if each night she fought a battle in her sleep. As if she were fighting to keep something out . . . or worse, to keep something in.

Memories flashed—horrifying convulsions racking her body, Mama's fear, the Church of Light exorcists with their fervent, shining eyes and merciless determination to drive the demons from her soul.

She shuddered from the awful memories and quickly sketched the sign of the Lord of Light. No, all things considered, now was a bad time for Ellie to go anywhere near the Fey and their powerful magic.

"Besides, I'm busy tomorrow," she told Lorelle, grateful for the genuine excuse. "Lady Zillina ordered an entire new suite for her receiving room, and Mama wants me to get started on the embroidery for the pillows."

"But, Ellie, the Feyreisen is coming!"

Ellie's breath caught in her throat. The Feyreisen? Despite her well-founded fear of magic, she'd dreamed all her life of seeing Rain Tairen Soul in the flesh.

Then common sense returned, and Ellie cast a stern sidelong glance at her sister. "Who told you that bit of silliness? Everyone knows the Feyreisen hasn't set foot outside the Fading Lands in a thousand years." Not since the end of the horrendous magical holocaust known as the Mage Wars.

"It's not silliness!" Lorelle protested indignantly. "I heard it straight from Tomy Sorris." Tomy Sorris, son of the printer, was the local town crier and usually well informed of the latest news and gossip.

Ellie was unimpressed. "Then Tomy's been smelling too much printer's ink." She transferred the punched down dough back into its rising bowl and covered it with a damp cloth.

"He has not!" A stamp of one small foot expressed the child's outrage.

"Well, perhaps he's just misinformed then," Ellie replied. If Rain Tairen Soul were coming, they'd have heard about it long before now. The Fey who'd once nearly destroyed the world in a rage of tairen flame wouldn't simply end his thousand-year exile without someone knowing about it in advance.

With a few quick swipes of a clean cloth, she swept the light dusting of flour off the tabletop into her palm and disposed of it in the waste bin beneath the kitchen sink. She cranked the sink pump twice and rinsed her floury fingers beneath the resulting cold spurt of water, and cast a glance back over her shoulder at Lorelle.

"Besides, why would the Feyreisen come here? He never had much use for mortals even before the Wars."

She recalled a story in yesterday's paper about a small caravan of travelers attacked near the Borders by *dahl'reisen*, the frightening mercenaries who'd once been Fey warriors before being banished from the Fading Lands for the darkness in their souls. Would Rain Tairen Soul come to Celieria because of that?

She dismissed the idea instantly. All her life she'd heard tales of *dahl'reisen* raids—such tales were so common they were used to frighten small children into behaving—but none of those stories had ever lured the King of the Fey beyond the Faering Mists that circled the Fading Lands. No, Lorelle must be wrong.

Ellie untied her apron and hung it on a wooden peg in the corner of the modest, cozy Baristani family kitchen and smoothed slender hands over her serviceable tan muslin skirts. Her shirtsleeves were bunched up around her elbows, and she tugged the plain cuffs back down to her wrists, unable to stifle a wistful sigh as she imagined a fall of ivory lace draped over her hands. It was, of course, a foolish daydream. Lace would only get dirty and torn as she went about her chores.

She smiled at Lorelle, whose pout had now become an outright scowl. "Come now, kitling, don't be cross. I'll take you to the park instead. It's bound to be less crowded, and we can still have a fine time."

Lorelle crossed her arms over her chest. "I don't want to go to the park. I want to see the Feyreisen."

Before Ellie could reply, Lorelle's twin, Lillis, came skipping into the kitchen, all atwitter. A mirror image of her twin, Lillis would have been indistinguishable from Lorelle except for the radiant excitement stamped on her face, which contrasted vividly with Lorelle's dark scowl. "Ellie! Ellie! Guess what!"

Ellie made a show of widening her eyes with exaggerated interest. "What?"

"The Feyreisen is coming, and Mama says you can take us to see him enter the city tomorrow!"

"Ha!" Lorelle exclaimed. "I told you so!"

This time the breath that caught in Ellie's throat stayed there. Tomy Soris might have sniffed too much printer's ink, but Mama was never wrong. Seeking confirmation, Ellie glanced towards the door.

"Mama? Is it true? Is the Feyreisen really coming to Celieria?"

Lauriana Baristani nodded, her fingers deftly untying the bow of her large brimmed sun hat as she crossed the threshold and entered the kitchen. There was a light of excitement in her eyes that Ellie had never seen before. "It's true," she confirmed.

Ellie watched in astonishment as her mother tossed her hat and woven shawl over the back of a nearby chair rather than hanging them neatly on the wooden pegs provided for that purpose. Her mother was a firm believer in a place for everything and everything in its place. Something was going on, something that had nothing to do with the unexpected ambassadorial visit from a twelve-hundred-year-old Fey who could turn himself into a tairen.

"Mama?" She picked up the hat and shawl and hung

them in their place. "What is it?" She gave her mother a searching look. Lauriana was a handsome woman in her mid-fifties, with a solid build and strong arms that could help her husband move heavy pieces of handcrafted furniture or hug her children close. She had the same rich brown hair as the twins, though her soft ringlets were threaded liberally with silver, and her eyes were a pleasant hazel. Her brown dress was neatly made of sturdy, sensible cloth, and her shoes were sturdy, sensible brown leather to match. But at the moment, she did not look sensible at all. She looked . . . *giddy*.

"Oh, Ellie, you won't believe it!" Lauriana reached out to grasp Ellie's hands. "Queen Annoura," she said, squeezing Ellie's fingers tight, "sent Lady Zillina to commission your father to produce a special carving in the Feyreisen's honor. He's to have it finished and ready to present to the Feyreisen at the Prince's betrothal ball!" When Ellie gasped again and the twins squealed, Lauriana beamed and nodded. "Commissioned by the queen. At last!"

"Oh, Mama," Ellie breathed. "Papa must be singing with pride!" After ten years as a master woodcarver, Sol Baristani had finally received a coveted royal commission. When word got out, nobles and rich merchants would be banging down his door to commission his work. Money, always rather scarce in the Baristani household, was sure to flow into the family coffers.

Lauriana flashed her eldest daughter a devilish grin. "And won't that just put Madame Rich and Snooty Minset's knickers in a twist?"

"Mama!" Ellie gasped, giving her mother a shocked look.

Her mother—definitely not her staid and sensible self—laughed out loud, then clapped a hand over her mouth. "Oh, that was evil. Just evil."

Ellie couldn't help laughing herself. It was so unlike her calm, unflappable mother to say something nasty, even about social-climbing Madame Minset, the banker's wife. Though if ever a woman deserved something nasty said about her, Madame Minset did—and that went double for her daughter Kellisande.

"But Mama, why is the Feyreisen coming to Celieria?"

Lauriana shrugged. "No one knows, but it's sure to be a spectacle. And I promised Lillis you would take her and Lorelle to see the Feyreisen." Ellie stared in surprise, and her mother blushed a little. "I know what you're thinking, and this doesn't mean I approve of Fey sorcerers. But, the Bright Lord did select Rain Tairen Soul as the vehicle through which He has delivered this latest blessing upon our family. I would not want Him to think us ungrateful. You will take the girls, won't you?"

Ellie glanced at Lorelle, who was now sporting a grin as large as a dairy cow, and had to laugh. "Of course I will," she agreed. The twins shrieked with happiness and danced about the kitchen.

No matter how dreadful her nightmares, Ellie would never have missed this once-in-a-lifetime opportunity to see the one and only Rain Tairen Soul. He was living history, the Fey who'd once, in a fit of grief-induced madness, almost destroyed the world.

How many ballads had been written about that terrible day? How many plays? Celieria's Museum of Arts held no less than twenty enormous oil paintings that commemorated the entire series of events, masterpieces painted by Celieria's greatest artists over the past thousand years. Ellie couldn't count the number of times she'd stood in front of Fabrizio Chelan's immortal, "Death of The Beloved," and wept at the unspeakable anguish the great master had depicted on the face of Rain Tairen Soul as he held Lady Sariel in her death swoon and cried out to the heavens.

To see Rain Tairen Soul in the flesh. It was more than she'd ever dreamed possible.

She wagged a finger at the twins. "You two had best plan to go to bed early. We leave at the break of dawn, so we can be sure to find a place with a good view."

Her mother shook her head. "You and your love of the

Fey." But for once, she didn't add her usual lecture about the evils of magic and the danger of temptations that wore a pretty face.

Though Ellie shared her mother's fear of magic, all things Fey had still fascinated her since she was a small child. "That doesn't mean I'm any less excited about your news, Mama." She reached out to grasp her mother's hands. "Indeed, I want you to tell me everything. What, exactly, did Lady Zillina say? Don't leave out a single detail."

Lauriana pulled up a stool and related the whole exciting event, including the ultimate pleasure of having Stella Morin, the neighborhood's biggest gossip, witness the whole occurrence. She'd come into the shop to tell Lauriana that Donatella Brodson, the butcher's youngest daughter, was officially contracted to wed the third son of a wealthy silk merchant.

"Oh," Lauriana snapped her fingers. "That reminds me. Den is coming for dinner tonight."

"Den?" Ellie repeated with dismay. Den Brodson, the butcher's son, was a stuffed pork roast of a young man. And ever since his first wife had died in childbirth six months ago, he'd been following her around like a starving hound on the trail of a juicy steak. He'd made a habit of catching her in dark corners, standing so close she could smell the reek of onions and bacon on him, and looking too intently down the neckline of her dresses as if he could see straight through the fabric to the soft curves beneath. His plump stubby fingers were ever clutching at her arm, as if he had some right to her. She shuddered with revulsion. She'd never liked him much, even as a child. Now he made her skin crawl.

Beside her, the twins rolled their eyes, and clutched at their throats, making gagging noises. They didn't like Den either.

"Mmm." Lauriana paid no notice to the rolling eyes and gagging faces, but she did shoo the twins out of the kitchen. "Go play in your room, girls." Then, to Ellie, "Wear your green dress, kit. It makes you look rather pretty."

"Why would I want to look pretty for Den?"

A stern hazel gaze pinned her in place. The laughing, flighty Mama was gone. Practical, no-nonsense Mama was back. "You're twenty-four, Ellysetta. That's long past time to be making a good match and starting your own family. Look at your friends. All of them long since married, with at least one child walking and another on the way."

"Kellisande's not wed," she reminded her mother.

"Yes, but Kellisande's not lacking for offers." The stern look in Lauriana's eyes remained the same, but her voice softened. "She's got beauty, girl, and wealth. You don't."

Ellie ducked her head to hide the glimmer of tears that sprang to her eyes. She knew she was no beauty. She'd seen her own reflection often enough to understand that. And Kellisande Minset had always been happy to point out her shortcomings in case she missed them.

"Even though you've got a fine, kind heart," Lauriana continued, "and a back strong enough to make any man a treasured helpmate, young lads and their parents don't look for those blessings first. The lads want beauty. The parents want wealth. The queen's commission will probably be enough to bring Den's family up to scratch, but you don't have the time to wait for Papa to make a fortune so you can take your pick of men." Unspoken was the common knowledge that if a girl was not wed by twenty-five, she was obviously defective in some way. Spinsters were to be pitied—and watched carefully lest the hand of evil that had blackened their futures laid its shadow over those around them.

Ellie couldn't believe what she was hearing. It was obvious her mother had already decided whom Ellie would marry. "But I don't love Den, Mama." To her horror, her voice wobbled.

"Ellysetta." There was a rustle of skirts and then the unexpected warmth of her mother's arms wrapping around her thin shoulders and drawing her close. "Ah, girl. This is my fault." Lauriana sighed. "I should have done my duty by you long ago. But you were such an . . . awkward . . . creature, and we were poor. I thought you'd never be wed, so what was the harm in letting you keep your dreams?"

Awkward. Such a mild euphemism for the fearful truth Mama never voiced. Ellie knew her parents loved her, as did Lillie and Lorelle. But that had not stopped her from hearing the talk of others—or seeing the fear that Mama could never quite hide whenever . . . things . . . happened around Ellie.

"But you've changed, Ellie, and so have our circumstances. You've grown rather pretty in your own way, and this royal commission puts a few coins in our coffers, with the promise of more to come. Look at me, child." Obedient to the command and the accompanying hand raising her chin, Ellie met her mother's solemn gaze. "Life is never certain, Ellie. This is your chance to wed, and you must take it."

"But, Mama—"

Lauriana held up a silencing finger. "Despite everything that happened when you were young, I've never curbed your love of Feytales or your dreams of truemates and happy endings, but that's for Fey, not mortal folk like us. We don't have centuries to wait for true love."

"I know that, Mama."

"Love will come in time, Ellie."

"But not with Den, Mama!" How could it, when the very thought of his touch revolted her?

"Hush! You've not even given him a chance, Ellysetta. Den's not a bad sort, and he's certainly shown interest in you these last few months. His family's well enough, both in manner and position, and your children would never lack for food. Believe me when I tell you there's nothing worse for parents than hearing a child cry for food they cannot provide. Even if that child is not of their own blood."

Ellie dropped her gaze as the reminder that she was not

the Baristanis' natural child knifed through her. Almost twenty-four years ago, on a journey from Kreppes to Hartslea in the north, Sol and Lauriana Baristani had found an abandoned baby in the woods near Norban. A girl baby with a shock of orange hair and startling green eyes.

Despite the fact that they were grindingly poor—Sol's hands stiff and nearly crippled by an accident that had left him unable to work as a journeyman woodcarver—they had taken in the baby rather than leaving it to die. And they had kept her, even while Sol barely eked out a living on pennies a week as an apprentice carpenter, his broken hands managing to hold hammer, nail, rasp, and lathe though they could no longer do the intricate detail work he loved. They kept her even when mysterious, violent seizures afflicted her and the priests declared her demoncursed. They'd even left Hartslea rather than cast her out or give her into the Church's keeping as the exorcists and the parish priest advised them to do.

After that, thankfully, their fortunes changed. Sol's hands had miraculously healed, and he'd been able to return to his first love, woodcarving. Ellie's ghastly seizures had dwindled, then stopped almost completely—a fact that Mama attributed to Ellie swearing her soul into service of the Light at her first Concordia in the Church of Light.

Still, Ellie had never forgotten all her parents had sacrificed on her behalf. Now there was a chance for Ellie to wed, if not well, at least well enough. It would ensure that Lillis and Lorelle would have the opportunity to make truly fine matches.

"You must trust your parents to do what's best, Ellysetta. For you and the family."

"Yes, Mama," she whispered. She owed them that much and more.

"I know he's not the man you've dreamed of, but give Den a chance. And if another young man of good family asks to court you, we will consider his suit as well."

"Yes, Mama."

"And wear your green dress tonight."

Ellie's shoulders drooped. "Yes, Mama."

That evening, Ellie donned her green dress and tried not to feel like a lamb being led to slaughter. At her mother's insistence, she wore Lauriana's bridal chemise beneath the green gown, and aged ivory lace fell over the backs of her hands, looking beautiful and feminine and delicate. Ellie wished she were wearing her own plain cuffs instead.

She stared hard at her reflection in the mirror. Startling green eyes stared back at her, looking too big in a too wan face, accentuated by prominent cheekbones and a long, slender nose. In the last year or so, her eyebrows and eyelashes had darkened to a deep auburn shade. The slashing wings of her brows were now exotic rather than pale and washed out, and once her eyelashes had darkened, their thickness and length had become quite apparent. She had been grateful for that, though at this moment she could have cheerfully wished them back to the transparent pale orange shade of her childhood. Her mouth was too wide, she acknowledged critically, her lips too full and too red. Her teeth, however, were white and straight, one of her best features.

She decided not to smile tonight—at least not so she showed any teeth.

She had ruthlessly subdued her wild tangle of hair into a knot on the top of her head, and for once was glad of its bright, unfashionable color. She hoped the hairstyle looked severe and unflattering.

She stepped back from the mirror. Unfortunately, Mama had been right about the dress making her look nice. The green color was flattering, and the bodice, laced tight to push up her breasts, made her look slender rather than skinny. She was still too tall to be considered feminine by Celierian standards. Flat-footed, she could look Den straight in the eye.

Ellie thrust her feet into her highest heels and immediately grew three inches.

Satisfied that she'd done exactly as her mother asked, and as much as possible to mitigate the attractiveness of her dress, Ellie left her tiny bedroom and descended the stairs to the family parlor.

Den was already there, sitting across from her father on one of Sol Baristani's finely carved settees and chewing a chocolate caramel with relish. His stocky body was clothed in what appeared to be a new dark blue plaid suit, cut just the tiniest bit too tight, with a yellow neckcloth tied in folds about his thick neck. A gold pin, shaped like a rather ungainly bear, glinted from the folds of the neckcloth. His brown hair, greased with a strongly scented pomade, was slicked back from his face, with a puff of curls carefully formed at the top of his broad forehead. His skin was ruddy, his nose partly flattened from a series of childhood scuffles, and his eyes were pale blue, rimmed with stubby black lashes.

He was attractive enough, in a rough, butcher's son sort of way. That wasn't what bothered Ellie.

He looked up, caught sight of her, and jumped to his feet, crossing the room to stand uncomfortably close to her. His gaze swept over her, then homed in on the swell of bosom thrust up against the delicate fabric of her mother's best chemise. A bosom that was three inches closer to his face thanks to her decision—poorly considered, she now realized—to wear high heels. His tongue came out to lick his full lips.

That was what bothered Ellie.

Fighting the urge to cross her arms over her chest, she forced a stiff little smile—no teeth—and said, "Good evening, Den. How nice that you could join us tonight."

"You look very pretty, Ellysetta." That came from Papa, of course. Den was still salivating over her bosom.

"Thank you, Papa." She was grateful for the warm love

shining from Sol Baristani's eyes. And for his presence in the parlor. The gods only knew what Den would have tried had they been alone. Judging from the look on his face, she wouldn't have liked it much.

"Mmm. Yes," Den agreed, licking his lips again. "Very pretty." His pale blue gaze traveled up her neck and paused for several seconds on her mouth. When finally he met her own gaze, there were spots of color in his cheeks.

For a moment she imagined she felt a disturbing hunger. His hunger, she realized, and it wasn't for food. Sudden panic roiled inside her, tying her stomach in knots, and making her break out in a clammy sweat. If he touched her, she knew she would be sick.

"Ah, Ellysetta. Good." Mama's voice snapped through the strange emotions that had captured Ellie, and she dragged in a gasp of air. No wonder she felt ill. She'd held her breath until she was dizzy!

"—to ask you to help me in the kitchen," Lauriana was saying, "but I've changed my mind. You look far too pretty to risk soiling your gown. Don't you agree, Den?" It was an embarrassing maternal attempt to draw a compliment from Den, but the young man didn't hesitate to oblige her.

"Indeed, Madame Baristani." Den bowed at the waist as if he were a Lord's son rather than a butcher's. "Ellysetta looks lovelier than I have ever seen her." The smug smile was back.

"Sol, perhaps you would give me a hand instead?" Lauriana gave her husband a pointed look.

Ellie's eyes went wide with panic. "I don't mind helping you, Mama!" She heard the shrill desperation in her voice. "Really, I don't."

"Nonsense. You stay here and entertain your young man. Your father is happy to help me." As they exited the room, Lauriana flashed an indulgent smile at Den and said in a coy, entirely un-Mama-like voice, "We won't be but a few chimes, children."

There was no mistaking her humiliatingly obvious

scheme, and Den was quick to take up the unspoken invitation. As soon as Lauriana's skirts disappeared down the hall, he stepped closer to Ellie, his square hands reaching for her. She stumbled backwards to escape his pursuit, only to find herself backed into a corner, trapped between his arms, staring in horrified revulsion as his thick, wet lips tried to attach themselves to hers.

Ellie escaped the kiss with a quick twist of her body, and tried to duck under his arm. She wasn't quite quick enough, and her slender muscles were no match for his solid bulk. After a brief, undignified tussle, she found herself back in the corner, pulled tight against his body.

"Come on, Ellie." His breath was starting to come a little faster. "We both know why your parents left us alone. There's no need to play the coy maiden. I don't want anything more than a kiss or two." He grinned, showing two rows of sharp and slightly crooked teeth. "For now."

"Den, we hardly know each other."

He laughed. "We've known each other since childhood, Ellie."

"But not like this . . . we've just been . . . er . . . friends." They'd never been friends. He'd been a taunting bully who liked to make her cry.

"I want to be more than friends now." His hands roved over her waist, and his lips descended, glancing off her cheek as she jerked her head away. His lips landed on her neck and stayed there, nuzzling. Something warm and wet touched her skin. Was that his *tongue?*

"Stop it, Den." She shoved at him, but couldn't break free.

His tongue explored her neck, then mercifully found its way back into his mouth where it belonged. She drew in a breath, thinking her ordeal was over, only to feel him—*biting? Was he biting her neck?* He'd pushed aside the collar of her chemise and was gnawing at a spot just at the base of her throat. A stinging pain made her yelp, then he sucked at the spot he'd just bitten, and once more that warm, wet tongue licked at her. Oh, gods, she was going to be sick.

Den drew back his head, looked at her neck, and gave a deep, satisfied chuckle. "I've been watching you for some time now, Ellie," he murmured, his voice thick and possessive. "Granted, you weren't much to look at as a child, all orange hair, freckles, and knobby knees. But lately, you've started to show a little promise." That smug, secret smile flashed again, and one thick-fingered hand came up to her neck to rub the spot he'd bitten. "I've decided to make you my wife, Ellie Baristani."

He didn't ask. He just said it, as if it were already an accomplished objective.

She gulped down the queasiness rising in her throat. "Den . . . you honor me," she managed to choke out, hoping to escape with what little grace she could. "I don't know what to say . . ."

"There's no need to say anything." And before she had a chance to escape, his mouth was on hers. His lips were wet and slippery, and that horrid tongue was on the loose again, this time trying to get inside her mouth. She gritted her teeth and shoved at his shoulders with all her might. She might as well have been shoving the side of a building. He didn't move an inch.

Without warning, one hand closed around her breast. Instinctively, she opened her mouth to scream. It was exactly the wrong reaction, and one he'd obviously been counting on. His hand shot up to hold her jaw open, and his tongue thrust deep into her mouth. Her screams, muffled by his mouth, came out as frantic little squeals that seemed only to excite Den further.

Never in her life had Ellie been assaulted this way. Where were her parents? How could they have abandoned her to this . . . this . . . mauling?

Beneath the revulsion and feeling of helplessness, a darker emotion burst into smoldering life. A wild, fierce anger. Her skin flashed hot and tingling, drawing tight as if something inside her flesh were struggling to get out.

Terror grabbed her by the throat as the room began to tremble.

Two hundred miles away, beside a campfire burning in the chilly night, Rain Tairen Soul felt a woman's emotions stab into him. Fear. Outrage. Desperation. He leapt to his feet, his nostrils flaring as if he could scent the emotions on the wind. His mind raced to find their path, to identify their source.

Another wave of feelings arrowed into him. Revulsion. Rage. Then stark terror. A wordless cry screamed in his mind. She was calling out to him. She was afraid and he was not there to protect her.

He flung himself from the ground into the sky, flashing instantly into tairen-form. Flames scorched the night sky and his roar of fury rent the air as he followed the path of the mind that called out to him in fear.

As suddenly and the call had come, it fell silent. Confused by the abrupt termination of the connection, Rain faltered in mid flight. His fury was still there. Licks of flame still curled from his muzzle and venom pooled in the reservoirs in his fangs, but his rage had lost its focus. The woman's fear and desperation were gone, no longer fueling his wrath. Banking right, he circled the sky and reached out with his mind, trying to find the one who had called. He found nothing but silence and the worried calls of the Fey warriors he'd left behind. Then the even more worried call of Marissya.

The warriors, he might have ignored, but not Marissya. All Fey men were bound to protect the females of their race, even from worry.

«Rain?» Marissya didn't try to hide the concern in her mental voice. She was a mere century older than Rain, had known him all his life. She was his friend. «What happened?»

«She called out to me. She was afraid.»

«Who?»

He hesitated. *«I don't know.»* Keen tairen eyes pierced the night. Far away in the distance, he saw the glow of Celieria. *«But I'm going to find out.»* He dipped one wing and banked again, heading towards the city in the distance.

Ellie sat at the dinner table and couldn't stomach the thought of putting food in her mouth. The terrifying anger and the disturbing sensation in her skin had passed almost as quickly as they'd come, with none but Ellie the wiser. Though she could have sworn the parlor had actually trembled, no one else appeared to have sensed it. Was she going mad now? Had the demons that had haunted her youth found a different, more subtle way to work their evil on her?

Ellie knew she must not let herself get upset. All her life, she'd worked to keep her emotions in check lest she accidentally trigger another seizure. She forced herself to take deep, even breaths, and filled her mind with calming thoughts.

Still, as she glanced at her mother from beneath her lashes, she couldn't quell a spurt of anger and resentment as Lauriana made pleasant small talk—small talk!—with Den Brodson. How could Mama even contemplate wedding Ellie to that odious *rultshart*?

Did Mama know what Den had been doing in the parlor? She had to have known. She'd made a series of intentionally loud noises before coming back in. What had that been all about except to let Den know he should stop his assault on Ellie? He had, thank the gods. With a final wet kiss and a last painful squeeze of her breast, Den had released her and said, "You'll do, Ellie." As if she were a haunch of beef he was approving from the slaughterhouse.

Ellie's relief at being freed had rapidly turned into a sense of betrayal. How could Mama know what Den had been doing and not be outraged? Surely Mama didn't know about that awful pink slug of a tongue.

Outrage and resentment clashed inside her. She was not going to marry Den Brodson. Not now. Not ever. Anger flared, quick and hot.

Suddenly, there was a feeling in her mind. A probing touch, as if someone or something was trying to reach inside her head. She had a distant sense of scarcely banked fury, and a stronger sense of something powerful rushing towards her with grim purpose.

Ellie's spoon clattered to the table. Everyone looked at her in surprise.

"Ellie?" Papa's brown eyes radiated concern. "Are you alright, kit?"

She put a shaking hand to her head. "I . . . I think so, Papa." The feeling was gone. Had it been her imagination? Another sign of impending madness? She forced a wan smile and tugged at the neck of her chemise. "I mean, yes. I'm fine. Just a little tired."

"What's that on your neck?" Lorelle was staring at the spot where Den had bitten Ellie's neck, the spot that Ellie had unwittingly just uncovered.

In an instant, everyone was staring at Ellie's neck. Embarrassed, she clapped a hand over the spot. She hadn't looked in a mirror. Had Den left a mark on her?

Apparently so, because her father was now staring hard at Den. That shameless *klat* just smiled his smug smile and met her Papa's gaze straight on. Mama's eyes darted from her husband to her daughter's suitor. There was a look in Mama's eyes that made Ellie's heart stutter. Embarrassment faded—even fear of what was happening to her faded—as worry slithered up Ellie's spine.

"Girls," Papa said. Ellie had never heard his voice sound so emotionless, so hard. "Go to your rooms." The twins jumped to their feet and scurried out. "You, too, Ellysetta." He didn't look at her, didn't take his unblinking gaze from Den's.

Ellie did not immediately obey. Had her parents not known what Den had done to her after all? Was it possible that they hadn't left her alone with him in the parlor for that very reason?

"Papa?"

"Go!" he barked, and Ellie all but fell over herself rushing from the room. Snatching up fistfuls of heavy green skirts, she raced for the stairs and took them two at a time, not slowing down until she was ensconced in the safety of her small bedroom.

Needing to know exactly what sort of mark Den had left on her, she went to the small dressing table tucked in the corner of her room. Her fingers shook as she struck a match and lit the oil lamp on the table. Soft golden light filled the room. Ellie leaned close to the mirror, tugging the neck of her chemise to one side to reveal a small, dark, oval mark at the base of her throat. In the golden glow of lamplight, the mark looked like a smudge of soot. She rubbed at it, but it didn't come off. She felt invaded somehow, violated, and suddenly very afraid of what was going on downstairs.

She sat on the edge of her bed, and waited. She didn't know how long she sat there. It seemed like bells before she heard the creak of the stairs and the slow clomp, clomp of her father's boots. She rushed to her bedroom door and pulled it open.

"Papa?"

There was disappointment and sadness in his eyes when he looked at her. "Go to bed, Ellysetta. It's getting late." He looked tired and worn. Old.

"But, Papa . . . about Den." What could she say? She couldn't very well tell her father about the embarrassing things he'd done to her. "I . . . I know Mama thinks he's a good match, but Papa . . . I don't like him. Please, I don't want to marry him."

Her father stared at her for a moment, then shook his head and turned away. "Go to bed. We'll talk tomorrow."

"But Papa—"

He just continued walking down the hall and into his room, closing his bedroom door behind him.

Ellie returned to her own room and undressed in shadowy darkness, hanging the green gown and her mother's chemise in the small wardrobe resting against the wall. She didn't want to wear either of them again as long as she lived.

After donning a cotton nightdress, she sat down beside the window and unpinned her hair. It spilled down her back in long, springy coils. Brushing it with steady strokes, she stared out at the night sky. Both the large moon called the Mother and the small moon called the Daughter were three-quarters full. It was a bright night.

Please, she prayed silently, fervently, hoping the Celierian gods would hear her. *Please send me someone else. Anyone else but Den.* She laid the brush in its place on her dressing table and crawled into bed, pulling the covers up to her chin and closing her eyes.

She didn't see the shadow fall across her room as the light from the Mother was blotted out by a large black tairen winging through the night. She didn't see the lavender eyes, glowing like beacons, turn their light upon the rooftops of Celieria. Searching. Seeking.

CHAPTER TWO

Beautifully and fearfully wrought, by dread magic
splendored,
With passion's fire his soul does burn, in sorrow his name
be whispered
—from the epic poem *Rainier's Song* by Avian of Celieria

Celieria's main thoroughfare was already lined four deep
when Ellie and the twins arrived at seven the next morning.
News that the Tairen Soul himself would be coming had
raced like wildfire throughout the city, and Ellie was con-
vinced that before ten bells every man, woman, and child
in the city would be lining the streets to ogle the legendary
Feyreisen, Rain Tairen Soul, the man-beast who had once
almost destroyed the world.

She sighed and began searching for a place from which
to watch the forthcoming spectacle. About halfway between the city gates and the royal palace, she found a
grassy knoll bordering one of the city's many small parks.
From atop the knoll, the children would have an unim-
peded view of the Fey procession.

Sending the twins off to play while they waited for the
spectacle to begin, Ellie spread her brown skirts and sat

down without a care for grass stains or the morning dew that dampened her dress. Her mind was still chasing itself in circles, worrying over what had passed between Den and her parents last night. She still didn't know. Papa had already been gone when she came downstairs for breakfast, and Mama had told her they would talk after she returned from the Fey procession. She couldn't shake the feeling that something very bad was about to happen.

Her sleep had been tormented by more dreams. Not the familiar, violent dreams of blood and death or the dark, malevolent nightmares that had haunted her most of her life, but new, frightening dreams of fiery anger and pale purple eyes, of a soundless voice that called to her, demanding that she reply. She remembered tossing and turning, remembered trying to block out those eyes and that insistent voice. Not until close to dawn had she finally found peace.

Now, staring up at the bright blue morning sky, with the Great Sun glowing like a huge golden ball, she could almost pretend that the dreams were nothing more than her imagination running wild. That worry about the situation with Den was to blame. That everything would be all right and life would return to its pleasant, comfortable routine.

She didn't believe it for a moment.

Twenty miles outside the city, two hundred Fey warriors and one Fey Lord traveled at a fast lope down the broad road that cut a swath through the Celierian landscape of lush fields dotted by little villages. Farmers and villagers bordered the road in small groups, having come as they always did with their families to see the immortal Fey run past. This year, however, their attention was directed not at the road, but overhead, where Marissya v'En Solande rode the wind on the back of a massive black tairen—the infamous Rain Tairen Soul himself.

The Fey had broken camp three bells before dawn and resumed their trek to Celieria at a fast clip. Marissya ran with them until Rain returned just as the Great Sun began to light the sky; then she continued the journey on tairen-back, allowing the warriors to resume their normal, easily sustainable run. They had traversed the next seventy miles in just under three bells.

All knew that something had disturbed Rain the night before and that he had gone in search of the source of the disturbance. But he had not spoken of it since his return, and not even Marissya could get him to talk.

When they neared the city, Rain landed, lowered Maris-sya to the ground, and shifted back into Fey-form. He paced restlessly as Marissya and the Fey prepared themselves for their ceremonial entrance into the city.

Marissya shed her brown traveling leathers for a red gown that covered her from chin to toe and a stiff-brimmed hat draped with a thick red veil that hid her face. Her waist-length dark hair was braided and tucked out of sight. The garb would have been hot and stifling had her truemate, Dax, not woven a cool web of Air around her. She was a *shei'dalin*, a powerful Fey healer, and none who were not Fey or kin were permitted to look upon her outside of council.

All around her, two hundred Fey warriors donned gleaming black leathers and spent at least half a bell pol-ishing and re-sheathing the dozens of blades each warrior wore when he left the Fading Lands. Her mate Dax, clad in the dark red leathers of a truemated Fey Lord, tended his own weapons with similar care. Though he was no longer of the warrior class—no Fey Lord was permitted to put his mate at risk by continuing to dance with knives—his blades would always stand between her and danger.

Marissya finished her physical preparations long before the men, and she went to join Rain. It had been many years since she'd seen him in such a state. He was restless, edgy, pacing back and forth with short, rapid steps. There was tremendous power in him, so scarcely contained that a shining aura surrounded him, flashing continuously with tiny sparks. His eyes glowed fever-bright. His nostrils quivered as if he were an animal scenting something in the air that set him on edge. If he'd been in tairen form, he would have been spouting flame. He was still in control of himself—she and all the Fey would have known if he were not—but he was in a high state of agitation and that did not bode well for the long day ahead.

She knew better than to touch him. One didn't touch raw power without receiving a shock. Instead, she reached out to him on their private mental path, the one they had forged centuries ago in friendship. *«Rain, be calm.»* She sent a soothing wave of reassurance along with the words, not surprised when he shrugged it off and continued pacing.

«She is there. For a moment last night I was in her mind; then I lost her again.» Frustration boiled through the link.

«Who, Rain? Who is there?»

He snapped around, eyes flashing. His long, elegant hands clenched and unclenched. His chest heaved. He was angry and frustrated, yes, but now Marissya realized it was more than that.

«She is,» he snapped. *«She! The one!»* And then, the one word she was sure to understand. The one word that explained everything. He shouted it out loud: *"Shei'tani!"*

There was a sudden clattering whoosh of sound, followed by absolute silence as two hundred Fey warriors jerked around to stare at their king in stunned disbelief.

Marissya's breath left her in an astonished gasp. *«But that cannot be.»*

«It can be nothing else.»

The tumult of Rain's emotions blasted over their mental link, and she stumbled back in shock, recognizing those feelings for exactly what they were. Her mind reached instinctively for her truemate, sharing the shocking truth of Rain's emotions with him.

Their gazes met across the distance, and as one they turned to look at their king.

He was pacing restlessly once more. Every few moments his head turned towards Celieria and the power in him burned a little brighter. They both knew the instincts driving him, knew that because he was the Tairen Soul, those instincts would be far more intense and far harder to control, fueled by both Fey and tairen passions combined. If they weren't very careful, the coming days could end in disaster.

As she caught sight of the Feyreisen riding the wind in tairen-form, Ellie acknowledged that just a glimpse of him was well worth the interminable wait and jostling crowds. Long before the actual Fey warriors drew near, Ellie and the twins saw Rain Tairen Soul soaring through the sky. He was all that legend claimed, and more. A gigantic, ferocious black feline with glowing purple eyes, frightening and beautiful all at the same time. He winged like a raptor over the city, circling again and again, emitting warning bursts of fire when the thronging crowd moved too close to the approaching Fey. Even from a distance, she could see the glistening danger of his sharp, venom-filled fangs. His ears were laid back on his head, his claws extended.

When the Fey warriors themselves came into view, the sight of them was almost equally as awe inspiring as the Tairen Soul. There were at least twice as many warriors as had ever come before. Row after impeccably formed row marched into view, and for the first time in Ellie's memory, magic surrounded them in a visible glowing aura of light.

A murmur of wonderment rose up from the crowd.

The Fey warriors presented a stunning display, clad in black leather from neck to toe and bristling with silvery swords and knives that gleamed in the sunlight. Every Fey warrior clutched two long, curving blades called meicha, and what seemed like hundreds of razor sharp throwing knives called Fey'cha were tucked into leather belts that crisscrossed their chests. If that weren't enough, each warrior also wore two massive long swords strapped to his back.

It was said that one Fey warrior was as lethal as ten champions. Looking at their fierceness, their precision, and the tangible glow of magic enveloping them, Ellie believed it.

In the center of the formation, surrounded by an even brighter glow, walked a single unarmed figure draped in voluminous folds of blood red. It was the *shei'dalin*, the Truthspeaker, Marissya v'En Solande, and the handsome, dangerous-looking man in red leathers by her side was her truemate, the Fey Lord Daxian v'En Solande.

As the procession moved closer, the crowd surged forward, everyone straining for a better look. Rain Tairen Soul roared and spouted a warning flare of fire. Accompanied by many screams and uplifted heads, the crowd wisely jumped back.

In the sudden shifting of massed bodies, Lillis lost her footing and fell to the ground. She howled in pain when Lorelle, trying to avoid being knocked over herself, trod on her hand.

Ellie was there in an instant, hauling Lillis to her feet and inspecting the injury. The child's little fingers were red, the skin slightly torn over one knuckle. "Oh, kitling. I'm so sorry. Would you like me to kiss it better?"

Lillis sniffled and nodded. "Yes, Ellie. You kiss the pain away better than anyone."

Giving her a fond smile, Ellie raised the girl's injured finger to her mouth. "Gods bless and keep you, kitling," she murmured and kissed the little finger. A tiny electric current leapt from Ellie to her sister, making them both jump. Ellie laughed a little. "Sorry, Lilli-pet. I didn't mean to shock you."

Rain Tairen Soul whooshed overhead, roaring, the sound like a clap of thunder in the air.

Ellie straightened in time for her to see the Fey come to

an abrupt halt, their curved meicha blades raised. The warriors immediately surrounding the Truthspeaker drew their long swords with a hiss of metal leaving scabbard.

The *shei'dalin* turned her head from side to side as if scanning the crowd. Beside her, her mate had razor-edged swords in hand and was ablaze with power.

The crowd went silent. From her vantage point on the knoll, Ellie watched with bated breath and clutched the twins to her side. She didn't have any idea what was happening, but it was something unusual. Something important and frightening. The crowd around Ellie began shoving, everyone trying to get a better glimpse of what was going on.

"Lillis! Lorelle! Stay close to me!" She grabbed the twins and hugged them tight, afraid they were about to be pushed off the knoll into the trampling feet below.

Rain Tairen Soul roared again, clawing the air, now obviously agitated about something. Flame seared the air, followed by another roar of tairen fury. From the street, the *shei'dalin* raised her arms and shouted, "Rain! *Nei!*"

The crowd began to panic, and so did Ellie. Someone stumbled heavily into her back. She staggered and tried to keep her balance, but her leather shoes slipped on the grass. With a cry of alarm, Ellie toppled off the knoll. She fell forward, pushing the children to safety with one hand and reaching out with the other to break her fall. She landed hard and screamed in pain as a man's boot heel stamped on her fingers, crushing the slender bones with a snap.

Pain and terror swamped her senses. People rushed madly around her, and another boot ground into her broken hand. She shrieked again. Barely able to think, certain she was about to die, she curled her body into a tight ball and brought her broken hand up over her head.

She was dimly aware that people were screaming around her. She didn't see Rain Tairen Soul fold his wings and drop like a hurtling black meteor towards the ground.

But something touched her senses, something made her realize that suddenly the sun was gone, and so were the people hurting her.

She glanced up and let loose another shrill cry of horror as the huge, terrifying black-winged tairen swooped down upon her, metamorphosing at the last minute into Rainier vel'En Daris Feyreisen, the infamous Rain Tairen Soul, who lightly stepped from sky to ground, one black booted foot at a time.

He towered over her huddled form. Death-black hair hung in long, straight strands that blew about his face in the windy remnants of the tairen's downdraft. His skin was pale and faintly luminescent, his face terrible in the perfection of its stunning masculine beauty, and his lavender eyes glowed with a brilliant, icy fire. With a wave of one hand, he threw up a towering cone of Air and Fire magic that surrounded the two of them in a whirling haze of white and red.

Ellie cowered in fear, instinctively holding up her broken hand to ward him away. With a sobbing gasp, she rolled to her feet and staggered back.

"Stay away!" she ordered hoarsely. Her heart was racing, her breath coming in fast, shallow gasps, but she couldn't seem to get any air. Had he used his magic to steal the breath from her lungs? She knew the Fey could do that sort of thing.

"*Ver reisa ku'chae. Kem surah, shei'tani.*" He spoke to her in a lyrical foreign tongue—Feyan, she realized, though she didn't understand the words—and stepped towards her.

"No!" she cried out. For all she knew, he'd just told her to prepare for her impending death. "Stay back! Don't come any closer!"

He paused for a moment, frowning. "*Ve ta dor. Ve ku'jian vallar.*" Then Rain Tairen Soul came towards her again, his steps slow and resolute. He reached for her, ignoring the way she sobbed and flinched away from him. His fingers, strong and surprisingly warm, curled around her forearms and trapped her with effortless strength. She had the overwhelming sensation of immense power, deep sorrow, and a terrible longing. But underlying all of those was another emotion, a violent swirl of rage. She cried out and struggled to free herself, succeeding only in grinding the bones of her hand together. Agony knifed up her arm.

A scream ripped from her throat. She fell to her knees. Unexpectedly, she found herself free. She blinked and risked a glance up at the Feyreisen.

His eyes were squeezed shut, his hands clenched in white-knuckled fists at his sides. He was shaking as if he were in pain. His eyes flashed open again. The ice was still in them, and confusion, and more than a hint of madness.

She watched him fearfully, her body poised to flee if he came towards her again.

With the flick of his finger, he fashioned a door in the whirling cone of magic. His voice, deep, ancient, commanding, called out in Feyan.

A moment later, the Truthspeaker stepped through the doorway, followed closely by her mate. The Fey Lord had sheathed his swords and as he stepped inside the cone of magic the Feyreisen had erected, his own glow of power winked out. He followed a few feet behind his mate as she approached Ellie.

Though the *shei'dalin's* face was hidden behind folds of red, she radiated waves of compassion and reassurance. Despite everything—including her own mind whispering that this was a Fey trick—Ellie felt her terror begin to abate. She needed to trust this woman. The Truthspeaker would never cause her harm. There was no need to be afraid. She could be calm. All would be well.

The soothing compassion, the compulsion to release her fear, was impossible to resist. Dazed, lulled by the powerful hypnotic spell of a Fey *shei'dalin*, Ellie didn't protest when Marissya reached for her broken hand.

The Fey's own long, pale fingers, slender and elegant,

passed over Ellie's. Warmth sank through Ellie's skin and into the flesh and bone below. Her pain evaporated. A strange, ticklish tingling spread across her hand, and she watched in astonishment as her bones straightened and knit. Within moments, her hand was whole and unhurt.

She flexed her fingers experimentally. There wasn't the faintest twinge of pain.

Ellie swallowed the lump in her throat and raised awestruck eyes to the Fey woman. "How did you do that?"

"Eva Telah, cor la v'ali, Feyreisa." The voice behind the veils sounded so peaceful, so soothing, so compassionate. Ellie wanted to sink into the comfort of that voice and absorb its tranquility. She fought off the lethargy with a brisk shake of her head.

"I don't understand you."

The Truthspeaker's head jerked up. Though Ellie couldn't see her eyes, she had a feeling the *shei'dalin* was staring at her in surprise. "You don't speak the Fey tongue?"

"Only a word or two." Ellie couldn't understand why that would be so unusual. Had she offended them somehow? "I'm sorry," she apologized. "I read it fairly well, but very few Celierians still actually speak your language."

"You are Celierian?"

Ellie blinked. "Of course."

The Truthspeaker cast a glance over her shoulder. The Feyreisen was still staring at Ellie, and he was frowning. She began to inch backwards. Immediately, the *shei'dalin* turned back to her, lifting her heavy veil as she did so. Huge blue eyes, so full of compassion Ellie could drown in them, were smiling at her from a face so beautiful it would put a Lightmaiden to shame.

"Be at peace, little sister," the *shei'dalin* murmured, and her hand came out to rest on Ellie's. "Of all people, you need never fear Rainier." As the Fey woman spoke, Ellie felt a faint pressure in her head, so slight she might not have noticed it had she not already been on edge. Her eyes widened as she realized the Truthspeaker was probing her mind. It was said a *shei'dalin* could strip a soul naked, leave even the strongest of men sobbing like infants. Truthspeakers could bend anyone to their will.

"No!" Ellie yanked her hand out of the Fey's grip and imagined a gate of brick and steel slamming shut around her mind, thrusting out the invading consciousness.

The *shei'dalin* gave a muffled cry and staggered back. The Tairen Soul's eyes flared bright, and a bubble of lavender light burst into glowing life around Ellie. A feral snarl rumbled from the Tairen Soul's chest, and he bared his teeth like a wild animal on the verge of attack. In a blur, he leapt between Ellie and the *shei'dalin*. In the same instant, the *shei'dalin's* mate also leapt forward.

«Get back!» The voice was in Ellie's head, sharp, commanding. Somehow, she knew it had come from the Feyreisen.

Scared out of her wits, Ellie pushed against the purple light enveloping her, trying to escape before the two Fey warriors decided to slaughter her where she stood.

Instead, to her utter amazement, the Tairen Soul whirled on the *shei'dalin* and her mate. His hands rose, power arcing from his fingers in blinding flashes just as the other Fey Lord's power snapped into blazing light and he sent a bright bubble of energy surging forth to wrap around his mate. Like his king, Daxian v'En Solande's teeth were bared in naked menace, but that menace was directed solely at the Feyreisen.

The two men faced each other, faces drawn in fury, power bursting around them, scorching the air with the scent of ozone.

"*Nei, Rain!*" the Truthspeaker protested. Her voice wasn't calm now. She sounded afraid. "*Nei, shei'tan!*" Then in Celierian, "I didn't mean to frighten you. Please, forgive me! Calm yourself. Guard your feelings."

It took a startled moment for Ellie to realize the Truthspeaker was addressing her. "*Me?*"

"Yes! Can you not see he is protecting you?" Even as she

spoke to the girl, Marissya sent a silent plea to Rain. *«I'm sorry, Rain. I didn't mean to frighten her. Please. She is un-hurt. See for yourself. Be calm. You must be calm. It is you who frighten her now.»* And to her truemate, whose thoughts and feelings she sensed as her own, *«Dax, shei'tan, I am not hurt. She only surprised me. It is my fault. I should not have probed her. She felt it and was frightened. Rain re-sponds to her fear, to protect her, as you protect me. Please, let go before someone gets hurt.»*

Neither Rain nor Dax relaxed his grip on his power or his rage. It wasn't surprising. A Fey Lord reacted violently to even the smallest perceived threat to his mate.

«Please, Rain. She needs you strong for her, in control of yourself. You must control the tairen in you. She was hurt, and you came. You protected her. She is safe.»

«She fears you.» Blazing half-mad lavender eyes pinned her. *«I will not permit it.»*

«I'm sorry. I—» The weave of Fire and Air appeared with-out warning. With incredible speed and dexterity, Rain had rewoven the protective cone of magic, shutting Marissya and Dax out, closing himself and the Celierian girl within.

It took Rain several minutes to beat back the tairen's fury, to shove it into a small corner of his mind and keep it there. Only then did he turn to face the woman whose emotions ripped at his sanity, her fear—of him, he knew, despite wanting to blame Marissya—tearing him in ways he'd never known. The web of Spirit he'd woven around her winked out as he released his power back to the elements. Still, she cowered from him. Rain would have torn out the heart of any other man who dared to frighten her so badly, yet he would not—could not—leave her.

"Come." His tone was imperious, yet the hand he held out trembled. "I could never harm you, *shei'tani.*" His Ce-lierian was rusty, deeply accented with Fey tones, and his attempt to appear non-threatening was equally out of prac-tice. The tairen in him still clawed at the edges of his control, all fiery passion, possessiveness, and primitive instinct. "I am called Rainier."

"I know." Her eyes were huge in the too-thin oval of her face. Twin pools of verdant green, they stared at him as if he were a monster. "You scorched the world once. It's in all the history books."

"That was a very long time ago." He tried to summon a smile, but the muscles in his face couldn't seem to remember how to form one. "I promise you are safe with me." His fingers gestured, beckoning her. "Come. Give me your hand."

The exotic flares of her brows drew together in a suspicious frown. "Why? So you can try to invade my thoughts like the Truthspeaker?" Rain could see she was still afraid, very afraid, yet she was working hard to master her fear.

"I . . . apologize for Marissya. She had no right."

"Then why did she do it?"

"She was . . . curious about you." She had done it to find answers, of course. Answers to the questions of how a Celierian child-woman could wield the power he had felt, and more importantly how she could possibly be Rain's *shei'tani*.

"Did she never think to just *ask?*" The asperity in her voice was unmistakable. Delicate, frightened *shei'tani* had steel in her spine after all.

"She will now. Believe me." The tairen in him was slowly subsiding. It had ceased pounding the door of its cage and was now pacing restlessly within, edgy but contained. For the moment. But it, like him, had a great need to touch this woman. Once more he held out his hand. "Come. Give me your hand. Please." The last was more a genuine plea than an afterthought. "I would give my life before allowing harm to come to you."

Ellie stared at the outstretched hand in stunned silence. Was Rainier vel'En Daris, King of the Fey, truly standing before her, vowing to sacrifice his immortal life to protect her? Her, Ellie Baristani, the woodcarver's odd, unattractive and embarrassingly unwed adoptive daughter? Surely, she was dreaming.

But this all seemed so real. And he was so beautiful. *Beautifully and fearfully wrought.* Her dazed mind supplied the quote from Avian's classic epic poem, "Song of Rainier." Avian, she now knew, had barely got the half of it. She had dreamed of Rain Tairen Soul all her life, and here he was. She felt herself moving towards him, her hand reaching out. He had asked, and she had to touch him. If only to be sure he was real.

Her fingers trembled as they slid into his. She trembled as his hand closed about hers. Warmth, like the spring heat of the Great Sun, spread through her body, and a sense of peace unlike anything she'd ever felt came over her. She heard him inhale deeply, watched his eyes flutter closed. A nameless expression, an unsettling mix of joy and pain, crossed his face.

He drew her closer, and she went without protest, dazed with wonder as his arms, so lean and strong, wrapped her in a close embrace. Her ear pressed against his chest. She felt the unyielding bristle of the countless sheathed knives strapped over his chest, heard the beat of his heart, and was oddly reassured. There was safety here, as there was no other place on earth.

She felt him bow his head to rest his jaw on her hair, the touch feather light. Tears beaded in her lashes at the simple beauty of it.

"Ver reisa ku'chae. Kem surah, shei'tani." He whispered the words against her hair.

"You said that before," she murmured. "What does it mean?" It sounded so familiar, like something she had heard or read somewhere before. She felt the stillness in him, the hesitation, and she pulled back to look up into his eyes.

His gaze moved slowly over her face as if he were committing her likeness to memory for all time. "I don't even know your name."

She blinked in surprise. Since the moment she had put her hand in his and he had pulled her into his arms, she felt like he knew everything there was to know about her. It was surprising and disconcerting to realize that, in fact, they knew each other not at all. "Ellie," she told him solemnly. "My name is Ellysetta Baristani."

"Ellie." Liquid Fey accents savored the syllables of her simple name, making it something beautiful and exotic. "Ellysetta." His pale, supple hand brushed the mass of her hair. His gaze followed the path of his fingers as they delved deeply into the untamable coils. "Ellysetta with hair like tairen flame and eyes the green color of spring. I've seen the mist of your reflection in The Eye of Truth." His gaze returned to hers, filled with wonder and regret. "*Ver reisa ku'chae. Kem surah, shei'tani.* Your soul calls out. Mine answers, beloved."

At last Ellie remembered why the Fey words seemed so familiar. She'd read them before in a slim volume of translated Fey poetry. It was the greeting a Fey man spoke to a woman when recognizing and claiming her as his true-mate.

The strange buzzing in her ears was all the warning Ellie received before her knees buckled.